Anthor

THE PARIS NOVEL

A Romance

ANTHONY MCDONALD

(Originally published as Gay Romance In Paris.
Anthony McDonald 2013)

Anchor Mill Publishing

The Paris Novel

Anthony McDonald

All rights reserved. Copyright Anthony McDonald © 2013 All rights reserved.

www.anthonymcdonald.co.uk

Anchor Mill Publishing

4/04 Anchor Mill

Paisley PA1 1JR

SCOTLAND

anchormillpublishing@gmail.com

The Paris Novel

For Tony Linford in memoriam, and for Yves Le Juen

ONE

I opened the windows that led out onto the balcony of my hotel room. We call them French windows. The French just call them windows. *Fenêtres.*

I stepped through them and was stopped in my tracks by the view across the street. In a window directly opposite two men of about my own age – twenty-seven – stood. They were in a sitting-room or salon. The blinds and curtains were open and the lights were on. The two young men were naked. They stood facing each other. About a metre separated them. Both their penises were erect.

I wasn't gay. But I was a writer. I was researching Paris. I'd never seen a scene like this before. I stayed to watch.

The two men moved slowly towards each other. Like ballet dancers. Actually they both had beautiful physiques. Perhaps ballet dancers was what they were. They had hair the colour of dirty gold, and their skin also looked golden in the light. They were exactly the same height. Which meant that when their two extended cocks met, a little before the rest of them did, they met exactly. Tip of foreskin to tip of foreskin. Like two pairs of little lips they seemed to kiss.

Then they embraced each other tightly. I'd seen men

do that before, obviously, although it wasn't something I often did myself. For some reason – and unlike most other straight men I knew – I didn't feel very comfortable with myself about it when I did.

They kissed of course. Tongues deep down each other's throat. I'd never seen men do that before, though of course I knew that some men did.

I have to say that I found them a beautiful sight. A man doesn't need to be gay to find Michelangelo's David beautiful. And because this whole book is about the difficult business of being honest with oneself, about learning to be honest, about trying to be, even if the process is a long one, I'll be honest about what happened next. I started to harden in my pants. And because it had just now got dark and there was no-one to overlook my fourth-floor hotel-room balcony I unzipped my jeans and took my cock out.

The two men repositioned themselves. One folded himself over the arm-rest of a sofa. There were two in the room. He was on the one that stood against the far wall, so he was in full-length double-curved profile from where I stood. The other came up behind him, spat on his hand and anointed his truncheon dick with it. Then, adjusting his height a little by bending his knees but still more or less standing upright, he entered his friend with a single, measured thrust.

I'd thought that these days all gay men used condoms. They didn't. I could see clearly enough to notice that. Perhaps they had both been tested, and never cheated on each other. I hoped so anyway. By now there was something I just couldn't not do. I started to masturbate.

The fellow doing the fucking started to come at the same time as I did. I shot my semen far out over the edge of the balcony, letting it fall who knew how or where or upon whom below in the street. Meanwhile the guy across the road climaxed inside his friend.

I didn't stay to see if they would follow up with a return match. Perhaps the young man who'd just been penetrated had already come on the sofa arm. I turned back into my room and shut the balcony French window behind me. I sat at the little desk the room was furnished with and began to write. Not about what I'd just witnessed. Not then. I'd come to Paris to be a serious writer, an acute observer of the social scene, not a mere voyeur. I'd come here to burn with a hard, gem-like flame, not turn into a peeping Tom.

I wrote instead about my arrival in Paris just an hour ago. About my first sight of the city since I'd last seen it ten years or so before, when I was in my mid-teens. I wrote this.

Paris. Winter. 1987.

It was the light, quite simply.

Roissy Charles de Gaulle, I discovered, was neither more nor less than a Heathrow Doppelganger or whatever the word for one was in French. Buying a coach ticket in that language (Etoile s'il vous plâit) elicited the price in English, the clerk not even looking up as he took the money, and although we set out towards the city on the right-hand side of the dual carriageway, it was raining in the desperate blackness of this February evening just as it might be, and by now almost certainly was, in England.

But the light was different.

Outside the périphérique, the ring-road that separates Paris from the rest of the world as ferociously as the vanished fortifications whose line it follows, light shone from poor bare rooms above corner bakeries now closed, from naked bulbs that dangled on suspect wires. Inside the périphérique's enchanted circle it came from warm lace-curtained windows, dripping from the thousand chandeliers that hung from sculpted ceilings in the avenue des Ternes. But whatever its source it had the same quality, this light remembered vaguely from a hundred paintings, that enticed from half open doorways, shining through the smoke of a million Gitanes, surviving its translation down the years from candle flame to gas, from gas to electricity: the yellowish, haunting, beckoning light of France.

I got off the bus at Etoile – the traffic system that circles the Arc de Triomphe. I went below ground and took a Métro train. That journey in the Métro provided one moment of shocking beauty when, in the blackness of the tunnel, the Eiffel Tower suddenly appeared at the window as if conjured. Its unmistakeable profile formed a glittering web of gold against the now diamond-studded darkness while at its feet reflections shimmered on the surface of an invisible river. It took me a few dazzled seconds to realise that my train had left its warren and was crossing the Seine high on a viaduct, its tunnel no longer a man-made one but an older one that merged with it: the night.

The Paris Novel

TWO

It was nearly seven o'clock. I would soon want something to eat. I checked myself in the bathroom mirror, and adjusted my clothing as the saying goes. I took the lift downstairs and stepped into the rue du Commerce. It was wet, cold, bleak and inhospitable. I made my way back to the Métro station at the end of the street. The line, having crossed the Seine only two stops back, had not yet returned underground but was carried aloft on an iron viaduct. The station was a greenhouse-like structure approached by a spiralling stairway. The whole effect was light and graceful: industrial architecture, and nineteenth-century at that, which had a feminine elegance unlike anything in London. I bought an orange card, passport to a month's unlimited travel in the city. I saw a beggar and gave him ten francs from out of the change. Then I climbed the stairs and caught a train.

Friends in England had told me that the best place to explore with a view to eating, drinking, night life and general Parisian atmosphere was the left-bank area around the Place Saint Michel. Others had sworn by Chinatown at the other end of the Quartier Latin. Flats were said to be cheap there still, should I feel like making it my permanent base. Yet others had recommended an early visit to the Marais, the only sizeable chunk of unreconstructed, pre-Haussman Paris still to be found on the right bank. For atmosphere, they said, there was nowhere, not even Montmartre, to touch it.

This evening I did not care where I went. I would let Paris decide for me. It was all right to let things take their course in this way from time to time, I thought, provided I kept it within bounds. Letting my shirts choose themselves as they appeared at the top of the pile in the drawer was one thing; applying the same principle to choosing a girlfriend, though, would be quite another.

Paris decided that I should get off the train, now underground again, when a station appeared whose walls were decorated with engravings of the old Hôtel de Ville, famously burnt to the ground during the 1871 Commune. I thought the pictures might be worth a look and then a comparison with the Hôtel de Ville itself, the 'new' one built a hundred years ago. With an impulsiveness that surprised me I leaped at the train doors and through them just before they snapped shut.

The sudden appearance of the Hôtel de Ville, white as an owl against the deep blue night, stopped me in mid-stride as I came up the subway steps. The whiteness, the coldness, the marble-slabbed open space around it, the floodlit formal fountains: the whole effect was like a gigantic ice sculpture so cold that it seemed to be lowering the temperature even in the surrounding streets. I fled the cold marble and the freezing fountains. I turned up a side street, turned two more corners at random. I was pleasantly lost.

I was in a narrow street of old stone houses, all different one from another, their individuality testifying to the independent spirits of their long-dead builders. Their shuttered windows were all at different heights and their crooked chimneys squirmed up from unexpected corners. Most of them had once had open arcades at street level and many now found room for a café or a grocer's, a restaurant or a tiny bar. One building in particular caught my eye, a dog's-leg twist of the road giving it the advantage of almost street-corner prominence. It rose just three storeys to its steep-pitched roof; an attractive building, but its large ground-floor windows, separated by green painted wood panels, were so filled with lace curtains and leafy plants that it was impossible to see in. A muted light shone out. Above the door a painted sign said boldly: *Bar Restaurant Le Figeac*. I pushed open the green door and went inside.

A dozen or so customers sat close together at very small tables where flickering candles wedged in old wine bottles shone through veils of cigarette smoke like harbour lights on a misty evening. An assortment of theatre posters and modern paintings hung on stone walls beneath a black-beamed ceiling. More surprisingly, there were birds. The window embrasures, each one a two-foot mortice piercing the ancient stone walls, were given over to them and, though it was night outside, they trilled and fluttered as I entered.

Just inside the door and to the left there was a small bar counter behind which an attractive young woman – petite, brunette, with a lively intelligent face – smiled a welcome. Behind her an open doorway led into the clattering kitchen.

The bar was only big enough for three people to stand at and two were already there. From the back, as I first saw them, they seemed alike: two men in heavy rook-black winter coats with hair above to match. The vermilion scarves that they both wore, brightly redolent of Moulin Rouge posters, and advertising their Parisian credentials more loudly than words, were the only concession their rear views made to colour. I came up alongside. Viewed from this new angle the two men appeared at once less crow-like and more distinct. The further one was about my age and good-looking in a rough sort of way. Streetwise, I thought. The nearer one might have been twice as old though he was only beginning to grey at the temples. His clothes had possibly been smart once, but it had been a long time ago. He wore an aggressively patterned tie whose width confessed the seventies. He had the beard, spectacles and furrowed forehead of the self-proclaimed intellectual; a copy of that day's *Libération* protruded from an outside pocket. He turned to me and, with a scowl, asked, 'Are you eating here?'

'Perhaps.' I had not yet made up my mind. I wondered whether the older man's next words would play a part in my eventual decision. Was he the proprietor, perhaps?

'Because, if you are, then beer,' (I had just ordered one), 'is no aperitif. No aperitif at all.' He glared frowningly at me and banged the flat of his hand on the counter to show his disgust. 'The hour for beer is past. Now is the time for pastis, unless you are like me whose liver can no longer support the stuff; then, *faute de mieux*, it's the time for kir.'

'Jean-Jacques...' said the young woman behind the counter, using the intonation with which a child's name is transformed into a gentle warning.

'Are you the *patron*?' I asked the bearded man. The woman and the younger man both smiled.

'No,' the man called Jean-Jacques answered, still frowning. 'Not even a shareholder.' His frown metamorphosed into a beaming smile. 'But I'm a very, very important client.' He turned his whole body towards the counter as he finished, just in case the woman should miss the point. Then he returned to me. 'Are you married?'

I said, 'No.' I had recently split up with my last girlfriend but I wasn't going to tell him that. I decided to match his forwardness with my own. 'What about you?'

Jean-Jacques peered at me. So did the younger man. 'I have a wife somewhere. Where exactly, though, I forget.'

'Take no notice of him.' The younger man leaned into the conversation, an expression of amusement beginning to animate his face. 'He talks nothing but *conneries* before nine o'clock and not much else after.' He made the sign, fist rotating on nose, for intoxication. 'You are not a tourist?'

'No.'

The young man nodded slowly, like a researcher whose most daring hypothesis has just been proved correct. 'I thought not.'

'Except tonight,' I said. 'I've just arrived in Paris to write a book but at this precise moment I don't know exactly where I am.' I was pleased with the way my French was coming back to me. I'd been considered good at it at school but it had suffered nine years of neglect since. I wondered if these two red-scarfed imbibers were typical Parisians. No doubt I would need to take a larger sample to be sure.

'You're in the Marais,' said the younger man.

'Not in the figurative sense, I hope,' said Jean-Jacques. Marais, I remembered, meant a swamp.

'But in the literal,' the younger one finished the sentence for his companion and then continued animatedly. 'You are in the exact heart of Paris. Paris has a heart, *et ben oui*. In times gone by she used to have a soul as well but now she has a liver instead.'

'Marianne,' said Jean-Jacques to the young woman behind the bar, 'Put a pastis for the Rosbif. You are a Rosbif, not a Boche? As I thought. And one for Dominique. For me another kir.'

'How do you mean, Paris has a liver?' I was working hard to keep up. I suspected I had just misheard. *Le foie* was liver, *la foi*, faith. It would be easy to make a mistake.

'The age of faith is dead or dying: the age of the liver being born.' Dominique capitalised on the potential wordplay. 'Our mortal livers exercise our anxieties as much as their eternal souls did those of our grandparents. Jean-Jacques here is a case in point. For him, kir is only venially sinful, pastis mortally so.'

'Ta gueule, Dominique,' said Jean-Jacques, who had clearly heard all this before. *'Arrête tes conneries.'*

'Thank you for the drink,' I said, and proposed their healths, privately drinking to what I thought a delightful idea: the vast, collective, metropolitan liver that was Paris.

The glasses emptied rapidly and I offered to refill them; the offer was accepted without any charade of hesitation or reluctance. 'Are you eating here, then?' I asked them. Dominique answered that he was not eating yet and Jean-Jacques's answer was delivered so firmly that it might have meant not just 'not yet' or 'not here' or 'not tonight' but that he never ate at all.

'Je mange pas,' was what he said.

The tables had been filling quickly during this time. I'd already glanced at the menu and liked what I saw. I asked Marianne if I could have a meal. 'There's only the big table left,' she said. 'Do you mind?' Why the size of the table should matter I could not imagine. Until I got there and saw that the table was a circular one, laid for six, and that five people already sat there in an animated crossfire of conversation. Too late now to withdraw, with Marianne already shoe-horning me into the narrow space, I took the sixth seat, and Marianne took my simple order.

Conversation at the table ceased abruptly. Everyone looked at me. 'I'm Peter. From England,' I said.

Seated on my left was a cheerful, uncomplicated looking woman with immaculately coiffed blonde hair and wearing a shimmering, chiffony confection of a yellow frock. She introduced herself as Françoise. It struck me that she was a little under-dressed for the end of February but this unseasonality was somehow cheering: it seemed to point towards a summer yet to come. As for other prospects, she was divorced (this came up quite early in the conversation) and I found myself taking careful sidelong looks at her when her attention was focused elsewhere. I concluded that she was attractive but a few years too old to interest me seriously.

On my right sat a younger couple, Jeannette and Denis. 'You've picked the best restaurant in the *quartier*,' Jeannette told me. 'I mean, for ambience. Not too many tourists and hardly any Parisians.'

I looked round at the busy scene. 'Then who are all these people?'

'People like us; people like you, for that matter. People who live in the *quartier*, people who work in Paris.'

'But not Parisians?' I was puzzled.

'Not real Parisians,' Jeannette explained. 'I'm from Troyes and Denis comes from Nantes. We both work in Paris. We met in this restaurant, actually. You may find it useful from that point of view yourself if you're on your own.' Denis and Jeannette had arrived in the *quartier* about six months ago, they told me. They still had about them that air of excitement and privilege that emanates from people who have just moved into a newly fashionable neighbourhood. In spite of myself I found I envied them just a little.

The other couple at the table, Régine and Fabrice, had been in the quartier for nearly two years. They weren't real Parisians either, they said. Régine came from Bordeaux and Fabrice from near Strasbourg. I put their ages at about thirty, a couple of years older than myself. They were a good looking pair. Régine was dark with large eyes, an oval face and ringleted hair: an almost nineteenth century kind of beauty. Fabrice's looks were of a more modern type. With luminous blue eyes and blond hair that was beginning to darken a little, the way honey does as it matures, he had an almost Nordic look about him. The look was enlivened by a real sparkle in the eyes and a humorous mobility about the corners of his sensitive mouth. This last feature was not at all eclipsed by a rather soft looking moustache which, like his eyebrows, was considerably darker than the hair on his head. How come we hadn't met before? Fabrice asked me. How long had I been living in the Marais?

'I don't live anywhere just yet,' I told him. I explained I was staying for my first few nights in a cheap hotel off the rue du Commerce, and that my visit to the Marais this evening was a matter of chance and impulse. 'It was the pictures of the Hôtel de Ville at the tube station,' I said. 'Does that sound silly?'

'An inspired impulse,' said Fabrice, leaning across the table towards me. 'Not silly at all.' He looked very intensely into my eyes at that moment. I wasn't sure I liked the way he did that. And yet somehow I did. Fabrice went on, 'You'll be looking for somewhere to live round here, I expect. Just the sort of place for a guy like you.'

'What do you mean, a guy like me?' I asked, a bit taken aback.

In his turn Fabrice now also seemed a little thrown. 'Oh, you know,' and his face flickered in the candle light. 'Someone on his own, new to Paris, bit of a Bohemian, that sort of thing.'

'Bohemian?' I choked slightly. 'I'm just trying to be a writer. Nothing very Bohemian about that.'

'Everything's relative,' said Régine. 'Fabrice is an investment banker.'

'And you?' I asked.

'Don't laugh. I'm in accounting. Cost control. But it is for a TV company.'

'Join the Bohemians,' I said.

'Seriously,' Fabrice came back. Again he had that

oddly intense look in his blue eyes. 'If you're really looking for somewhere to live round here, I could put you in touch with someone who might be able to help. And you'd get to meet a real Parisienne into the bargain.'

'You mean I still haven't met one?' I turned back to Françoise. 'Surely you...'

'I was born in Paris, it's true,' she admitted, her yellow dress rustling in sympathy, 'but I'm not really one of them. My parents were from the provinces. Parisians are the end. I have a small dress shop here and I meet them all the time. If I told you how they behaved you would never believe me.'

'She's right,' said Jeannette. 'They're so rude.'

'Ils se foutent des autres,' they all agreed. The Parisians, it appeared, did not give a fuck about other people.

'Anyway,' said Fabrice, 'I'll give you an introduction to La Belle Margueritte. She's a cousin of a friend. Rumoured to be *assez riche*. She's the owner of a pretty big *immeuble* just a couple of blocks from here. She might find she had a small half-forgotten apartment going cheapish – if she decided she liked your face.' Fabrice paused and shrugged non-committally. 'And there's no reason why she shouldn't.'

'There,' said Françoise as she extracted a particularly recalcitrant snail from its shell, her voice full of triumph. 'You have a *tuyau* already.'

'A pipe?' I queried. My understanding was still anchored to the concrete meanings of the words.

'A piece of useful information,' explained Denis. 'For example, someone in the know tells you which horse to put your money on. That's a *tuyau*.'

A litre bottle of Côtes du Rhône had circulated among us and been quickly disposed of. A second had been ordered while I was still on my *saucisson* starter and my glass was being refilled as a matter of routine by the others as soon as it was empty. How the bill would be divided I could only guess.

At nine o'clock precisely a plump woman in late middle age entered the restaurant carrying a basket full of fresh baguettes. 'It's Madame Touret,' Denis said, his voice hushed with respect.

I half expected the men to stand and salute. 'Who is she?' I asked.

There was no need for an answer. Madame Touret moved between the cramped tables with an agility that belied her waistline. Shaking a hand here, exchanging a word there, she circulated among the customers with the practised assurance of a royal personage. I was presented to her. She hoped my stay in Paris would be a happy one and my visits to the Figeac frequent. She passed on, a swirl of smiles, into the kitchen. Madame Touret was the owner of the restaurant.

'Her family came from the town of Figeac in the Lot,' said Régine, as if to forestall questions about Parisian origins. 'Hence the name of the restaurant. The chef, René ... have you met him yet? ... he's her son.'

Emboldened by the simultaneous arrival of my entrecôte à la Bordelaise and a third bottle of wine, I asked about the two men at the bar. For Dominique and Jean-Jacques still stood there all this time in animated discussion about something or, more probably, nothing very much.

Jeannette and Denis did not know them. The others were happy to put them in the picture. 'Dominique does a bit of everything,' Fabrice said. 'Odd jobs, selling things. Does some work as a film extra sometimes. And if I said he was a drugs dealer as well you'd get the wrong impression but – and this is another *tuyau* – if you were ever looking for an occasional supply of marijuana, he's probably where you'd start.'

I had smoked nothing so interesting since leaving university and only rarely then. I appreciated the tip less for its usefulness than for the friendliness that prompted it. I began to feel accepted in the foreign city.

'As for the other one,' Fabrice went on, 'Jean-Jacques is supposed to be a poet. I say 'supposed to be' because I've never seen any evidence for it. As far as I know his work at the bar keeps him busy most days and his muse is a liquid one.'

A hatchet-faced man at the next table turned round at that moment and tapped Fabrice on the shoulder. 'I couldn't help hearing what you said and I'm obliged to correct you. The gentleman you speak of is indeed a poet, a published one and well known in his day. And though you are certainly too young, monsieur, to remember this, he played no small role at the barricades of sixty-eight.' He returned to his own conversation. Fabrice looked suitably chastened.

'You learn something new every day,' said Françoise brightly, and poured some wine into Fabrice's glass as if in token of her support.

With the arrival of the fourth bottle I felt not just that I would like to live in the *quartier* but that I already did. During the cheese I remembered with a flash of panic that my hotel was on the other side of Paris. But over the coffee, and more especially the cognac that arrived with it, I decided that didn't matter in the least.

THREE

I wasn't the first to leave the table. Jeanette and Denis went home first, then Françoise. At that point I made a move to get up and go, but Fabrice begged me to go with him and Régine to a nearby little bar they knew. He had such a puppy-dog look on his face that I didn't have the heart to say no. The next day was Saturday anyway. There would be no work for Fabrice or Régine, and as for a writer like me ... well, I could make up my schedule as I went along.

In the end Régine didn't come with us. It was late, she said, and she'd had enough wine for today. 'But you two go and be boys together,' she said. 'Have fun.' As we left we passed the two black-coated men still standing at the bar. Jean-Jacques and the younger Dominique. We said goodnight politely but they took no notice of us.

We 'boys' both kissed Régine on the pavement outside the restaurant, then she made her way towards their apartment. It was little more than a hundred metres away.

As for the bar that Fabrice took me to, The Little Horseshoe was even nearer to the Figeac and just about in sight of it. It owed its name to the size and shape of the counter which almost filled the cramped interior. There was just room for a semi-circle of customers to stand round it and for one very small table in each of the four corners. Its appearance – well-worn woodwork, smoke-darkened ceiling and a polished brass rail around the bar – had probably not changed in the past century. It was packed solid.

Fabrice ordered us a small beer each. We clinked glasses. Because of the crush in the place, we were leaning shoulder to shoulder over the bar. 'Welcome to Paris,' Fabrice said. 'It's good to have you here.' With our faces turned towards each other we were almost close enough to kiss. Not that I had any thought of doing that, but I couldn't help remembering the two men I'd seen earlier. That wasn't something I'd forget in a hurry. I remembered they'd both had dull gold hair. Fabrice and I were, by coincidence both dark blond, though Fabrice was rather taller than average height and I was somewhat less. I was very surprised just then to feel my dick give a little twitch in my pants.

We had one beer, then Fabrice said, 'It's very crowded here. Can I take you to another place, just a short walk away, where we'll have more space and can sit and talk?'

Had Fabrice not had a girlfriend, one whom I'd met and just spent the evening with, I'd have said no to that. I'd have made the obvious deduction that here was a gay man who was trying to pick me up. But he did have a girlfriend, and so I said yes.

And so I found myself meandering up the rue Vieille du Temple with Fabrice, looking for another bar which, so he said, had the advantage of staying open all night.

At that hour the rue Vieille du Temple was a dark,

forbidding place and when we turned off it into a labyrinth of alleys it seemed that the Marais had thrown off its daytime identity and reverted to an older one, medieval and sinister. As we threaded our way through the ill-lit maze I wondered how I would ever find my way home and, in a momentary reassertion of my usual disposition, cursed myself for being so easily led into an adventure such as this.

We stopped at a solitary lighted window and knocked at the door beside it. *'C'est qui?'* a voice enquired.

'Fabrice et un Rosbif.'

Bolts were withdrawn and the door opened. In contrast to the Little Horseshoe this place was large and bare. The walls were the explosive red of overripe tomatoes and the ceiling a shade of brassy, snakeish green. The lights suspended from it were shaded with the kind of tasselled fringes that seem designed to maximise the accumulation of dust and minimise the diffusion of light. A billiard table stood morosely at the far end of the room, one neglected cue lying on its green baize. The scene reminded me vaguely of a picture I'd seen somewhere, but in the state I was in by then I couldn't place it. Nearer at hand only one of the plain wood tables was occupied by customers. A group of middle-aged men sat there with glasses, a bottle and dominoes. The light gave them something of the appearance of vultures. It seemed they knew Fabrice. We joined them.

Introductions were perfunctory, names being exchanged only to be immediately forgotten, and we new arrivals were assimilated into whatever drunken game of dominoes was in progress. Someone placed a domino on its edge on the table. The next person put another one nearby, and the next two dominoes formed a bridge across the top. Turn by turn, more dominoes were added until a tower was formed. It seemed childishly simple. I wondered that there was no more to it than that. As the tower increased in height it grew more difficult to keep it stable; the upright dominoes had to be placed nearer and nearer to the centre of gravity. At last the only way upward lay in the alternating of one horizontal with one vertical domino and after two courses of this the whole edifice swayed, toppled and collapsed.

'Tournée générale,' said the man whose last domino had delivered the fatal blow, and put his purse on the table. The object of the game was revealed.

A clear colourless liquor was served. It tasted of apricots. I could only guess that it was strong. A second tower was started. This time it did not get so high and it was my ill-judged domino that sent the structure clattering to the table top where my money had then to join it. I lost count after that of the number of towers, the number of rounds of apricot liquor, noticing only that they succeeded each other more and more quickly like the passing years.

Fabrice asked our older companions if they knew Jean-Jacques. They did. Was he really a poet? he asked. A first-rate poet, they all agreed, as far as poets went. Someone said maliciously that he had sold his liver to the devil in return for good reviews for his first volume of verse. The devil was expected almost any day now to come and claim what was his own, hence the poet's recent abandonment of pastis in favour of kir. They all shook their heads. Kir was considered a sell-out.

My memory of the evening now degenerated into glimpses, as when a sea mist briefly parts to show a pale tableau of sails and sea and shore. One of the more vulturine of my companions took it upon himself to build his own domino tower. 'I shall now show you the hope of the world,' he announced when it was about seven storeys high. A joint was circulating now and the room was in soft focus. I watched, hypnotised, as the speaker withdrew two horizontal dominoes from about halfway up, like someone perversely removing tins from a supermarket stack. But the tower did not collapse. It dropped a half centimetre and swayed slightly but it stood. The builder placed the two dominoes upright on the top with a theatrical flourish. 'That is the hope of the world,' he said. 'There is no other.'

The mist came down again.

Fabrice didn't get the chance to have the quiet chat with me that he'd seemed to want. But I did occasionally think I felt his knee rub against mine beneath the table as we sat side by side. It could have been an accident though, or I might have imagined it. I think my brain had been a little over-stimulated by what I'd seen those two men doing earlier in the evening.

I began to think it was time to go, and said so. Fabrice rose to his feet. 'You're right,' he said. 'But don't try getting back to the rue du Commerce at this time of night. We've a sofa. Stay with us.'

What could I do except say yes?

Our departure was hardly noticed. Our last sight of the group was from the doorway. Two were trying to turn the dominoes into a model battleship but were unable to agree which end was the stern and which the bow. The third was fast asleep, his head on the table like the dormouse at the Mad Hatter's. Had the others later attempted to squeeze him into the empty apricot liqueur bottle I would not have been surprised.

I was surprised, though, to find that I felt good with Fabrice, lurching a bit as we retraced our steps.

*

'In principle I don't let. You must understand this.' Margueritte d'Alabouvettes sat in an armchair opposite me, her legs elegantly crossed. She was a still attractive woman of about fifty. Her poise, perhaps her willpower, made the studio apartment seem bigger than it was. 'But to a friend of Fabrice...' She smiled coolly. 'Do you smoke?'

'Only just occasionally, to keep a lady company,' I said.

Madame d'Alabouvettes flushed slightly. I was in two minds about my answer. Had I been gallant or merely fawning? In the end the feeling of satisfaction at finding the right words in French and managing to trot them out so quickly overcame my scruples. I allowed myself to feel pleased. Things were going well. I was still hungover from the previous night, and my sleep on Régine and Fabrice's sofa had not been the most comfortable of my life... But I felt I was making friends here, and Fabrice had been as good as his word in giving me Margueritte d'Alabouvette's phone number and address.

'Ordinarily I keep these studios for the use of my family and friends when they are visiting Paris,' she continued after we had both embarked delicately on menthol cigarettes. A lifetime of producing oboe-like vowels of the finest quality had given her the slightly protruding lip structure that is shared by people in the act of whistling and members of well-born French families. I was conscious of being in the presence, at last, of a true Parisienne.

'Most of the rest of the building is in the hands of my manager who deals with the office space lettings. I keep only two flats for my own personal use on the first floor. And there is my daughter's flat on the second floor and my second son on the fourth. My eldest in on the third and the third is in Paraguay. You see, we are a *famille nombreuse*.'

'It must be nice to have so many of your family around you,' I suggested while I tried to sort all this out.

'Around me?' She did not understand at first. Then she did. It was I who had not understood. 'Oh no,' she said, 'I don't live here. I am normally in Barcelona and for weekends, Rome. In Paris I'm only ever passing through. My husband travels so much, you see. London and Los Angeles.'

'I see,' I said, though I did not.

'I do hope you will like Paris. For me, no. I know it is full of beautiful things and places but the Parisian is someone who gets on my nerves. You know them of course. The nouveau riche women in the sixteenth who wear silk gloves to go to the supermarket. Those red berets and that forties-style make-up. So bourgeois. And they don't care, you know. *Ils se fichent des autres.*'

'You are not a Parisienne yourself?' I felt a twinge of disappointment, cheated of my promised example of the species.

She looked slightly shocked. 'I was born here, of course,' she allowed, 'but the family is from the Haute Savoie, further from Paris, you must admit, than Brussels is or London. We still have a little property there: a small manor house and a few farms. You must come and stay with us down there some time if you have a holiday.'

I began to realise that, if I had failed to bag a real Parisienne, I had at any rate encountered a specimen of an even rarer breed: the seriously rich.

'You do understand,' she continued with no change of tone, 'that you will have to pay cash.'

'Fabrice did mention that.'

'You see, I have no bank account in France to put a cheque into. There, I knew you would understand.'

A tour of the apartment was conducted swiftly. We discussed the electricity bill and the vagaries of the cooker. We smoked a second cigarette. We negotiated a price. I was nervous at doing such a thing in French but I found the cigarette seemed to help. Perhaps it was not for nothing that tycoons and movie moguls were always depicted smoking cigars.

'On no account let Monsieur Guyot know that you are paying rent. If anyone should ask, explain that you are a cousin. Perhaps, now that I think about it, it would be better if you did not put your name by the bell-push. Or if you do, write it very small. It is always easy to explain in advance to visitors that the bell is at the top on the left.'

I said yes to all of this. I did wonder who Monsieur Guyot was, and I was certain that explaining in an English accent that I was a cousin of the d'Alabouvettes would replace a small suspicion in the mind of anyone who was curious with a rather larger one. But something told me not to question. The meeting was going very well even if its momentum was generated by an engine unfamiliar to my English way of dealing.

We met the concierge at the bottom of the stairs. She was a woman not much older than I was. That surprised me; I had expected a crone. 'This is Luisa,' said Margueritte d'Alabouvettes.

It was arranged that I would move in, with the cash, this very afternoon because, although the next month did not officially begin until Tuesday, my new landlady would be flying to Los Angeles later tonight and would not be returning to Paris for a month. I had been lucky to catch her between hops. She wanted the rent in advance and could hardly keep me out of the flat once I had paid it. So my first two nights in the studio would be a kind of present. As to what Margueritte would do with the French francs in Los Angeles, I was too discreet to enquire.

Luisa showed me out into the street. She caught sight of someone across the road, a lanky young man with a mop of dark hair, and called to him. 'Joe.'

'He is an American man,' she explained to me while he crossed the road towards us. 'He lives two streets away. Perhaps, with a language in common, he will be a friend for you.'

I doubted that very much. Why do people seem to think that if two foreigners share a common language they are bound to be friends?

But I was wrong and Luisa was right. By the time the American guy had crossed the road, and we'd been introduced, and he'd shaken my hand and smiled at me, my defences had been breached. I found I couldn't not like Joe.

FOUR

'You got time to go for a coffee?' Joe said almost as soon as Luisa had retreated behind the huge varnished street door and shut it with a clang.

I said, 'Why not?' Joe led me abruptly down a side turning, in the opposite direction from the one I already knew. He seemed to pause at the door of a café. I said, 'Are we going in here?'

'No, not that one. *They* use that one. We'll go across the road.'

'I see.'

Joe took out a packet of Gitanes. 'Smoke?'

'Occasionally....'

'Mind if I...?'

'Go ahead.' I don't think he'd heard my previous answer.

'Hey, look out! We drive on the right, you know.'

'Thanks.' I'd been distracted by the Eiffel Tower, which now appeared to be striding into the street to meet us as we crossed. 'Who are *they*?'

'People we don't want to meet. Different ones different days.'

I accepted that. It made a kind of sense.

'You know what?' Joe looked at his watch. It was well after midday. 'Let's have a beer.'

We went in and stood by the zinc-topped counter. The café was not very full but an impression of frantic activity was given by the urgent sounds coming from the espresso machine and by the manic pace set themselves by the waiters. A barman approached us, shook hands with Joe, was presented to me, exchanged pleasantries and then hurried off to serve another customer who had arrived after us and was calling loudly for a pastis.

'This'll take a bit of getting used to,' I said after five minutes had passed and I'd been introduced to two more waiters without Joe managing to secure us a glass of anything.

But good things take time. *'Deux demis,'* Joe was able to command at last. 'Draught beer OK for you?' I said it was.

'So what brings you to Paris?' Joe asked. 'Cheers, by the way.'

'Cheers. British Airways brought me.' I realised at once that must have sounded rude to someone who had just bough me a drink. But I wasn't sure how much I wanted to tell this rather forward if likeable stranger. I said, 'I've come to write a book.' But that was all I was ready to give away at this stage. I threw the question back. 'What brought you here? It's a hell of a lot further across the Atlantic.'

Joe looked straight at me. 'Love,' he said. 'Love brought me here and love left me here and now my job keeps me here. *C'est comme ça.*'

'I see,' I said, unsure whether Joe was sending me up or sending himself up or just being honest and commendably brief. 'Should I congratulate or commiserate?'

'Neither. That's just the way it is. Enjoy your beer. And then enjoy Paris. Why do you think any of us are here? All of us Yanks and Limeys and Aussies and Paddies? Get to know any of the ex-pats here and you'll find the same thing: there's always a story behind their being here. More than meets the eye.'

I asked him about his job. He was a teacher of English, he said, in one of the larger business language schools. Then he looked very intensely into my eyes, the way Fabrice had done several times the night before. Was that something everyone did here? I supposed I'd get used to it.

Joe said, 'You're looking a bit rough, I have to say. Hangover perhaps?'

I burst out laughing. 'No,' I protested. I thought for a second. 'Oh all right, maybe a little bit. I overdid the French experience a bit last night. Spent the night on a sofa on the other side of the Marais and found today a little bit uphill as a consequence.' I gave him an edited account of yesterday evening.

Joe drummed his fingers of the side of his glass of

beer. 'Couple of these at five o'clock's a great idea but you do have to give it a break before bedtime. Otherwise you're not going to make it through your first week. So tell me, anyway: who did you sleep with in the Marais?'

To my surprise I didn't feel offended by this but laughed before replying. 'Sorry to disappoint you but I didn't sleep with anyone. I stayed with a charming couple called Régine and Fabrice.'

'You didn't do bad for a first day. Your French must be pretty good.'

'It's not great but it seems to be improving very quickly. I noticed it got better during dinner.'

'Everyone notices that. You'll find it goes on improving for about two years. After that you won't bother any more. Eventually, if you see a verb you don't know, you presume it's something you do with ropes on a ship and you don't need to learn it. Least, that's what I found. Anyway.' He hopped onto another subject like a bird popping from twig to twig. 'It'll be nice to have you as a neighbour. And you're lucky to have got a place so fast. Sounds like you're lucky to have met this Fabrice guy. Most people arrive, look six months for a one-person studio, then the day they find it, bang (if you'll excuse the expression), they meet the partner of a lifetime and have to start over, looking for a place for two. With me it was exactly the reverse. Six months to find a love nest that was meant to be for eternity then out on a limb to look for a perch for one. *C'est comme ça.*'

'And how long have you been in Paris?' I asked him.

'A long and instructive three years. You'll come round for dinner one night. I have two plates and two forks so there wouldn't be a problem. Have you always had a beard?'

Instinctively, my hand went to it. It was a full beard, but I kept it short, almost like extra long designer stubble. It was black, like my eyebrows and lashes, and so created a striking contrast to my blond hair. I knew I looked good with it. Especially with the 'bright blue eyes' people always told me I had. I knew it worked a treat with the girls anyway. 'Always?' I said. 'Not always.' I could be as obstructive as anyone when I wanted to be.

'You knew what I meant.'

'I grew it when I was nineteen in order to look my age,' I said. 'One day I suppose I'll have to shave it off in order not to.'

'Pity. It suits you.'

A few minutes after that he looked at his watch and said it was time to be running along. He gave me his address and phone number and I gave him the ones that would be mine in a few hours. He renewed the dinner invitation for 'some time real soon' as he got up to go, then left the café, a lanky figure moving among the tables in a way that reminded me again of a bird, this time a wading bird perhaps.

A few minutes later I left the café, and took the Métro back to the rue du Commerce to pay my hotel bill and get my stuff. Before leaving my room for the last time I went out onto the balcony and peered at the window opposite. Nothing was going on there. I felt oddly cheated by that.

On my way back to the Métro I met a beggar again. Was it the same one as yesterday's? It was difficult to be sure. I gave the man five francs.

*

By the time I'd unpacked my stuff, or some of it, it was evening and already dark. I left the handsome building I'd just moved into and turned left towards the Figeac. After all, I would have to eat somewhere before bedtime even if I couldn't run to a meal on yesterday's scale every night. But – to be honest – I also had the only half admitted hope of running into Fabrice.

Instead, when I pushed the door open, I found the poet, Jean-Jacques, alone at the bar reading *Libération,* which he had spread right across the tiny counter. The overhead light, shining through the glass of kir that he had placed on top of the paper, cast a rosy glow over the day's news. He turned to stare at me. 'Haven't we met somewhere?' he growled.

Marianne, emerging from the kitchen, heard him. She looked at me, remembered me from the night before and smiled. 'The alcohol's ruining his memory,' she said. 'Switching off the brain cells one by one like the lights

The Paris Novel

of the Tour Montparnasse when the workers go home. One day it will be all dark.' She turned to Jean-Jacques. 'Have you forgotten already? This is Peter who was here last night.'

'Very possibly,' he answered. 'What will you have, Rosbif?'

I glanced round the room instinctively, though trying not to let Jean-Jacques see me doing it. Trying not to let him see my disappointment that I had only him for company. None of my other, younger acquaintances were there. No Régine, no Fabrice. No doubt they, like me, would not normally eat out every night of the week. Suddenly transformed in my own mind into an *habitué*, I felt a quite unreasonable resentment against the strangers who peopled the restaurant tables. I returned my attention to Marianne and the poet, and told them I was shortly to become a neighbour. They made appropriate noises. Where exactly was my new flat? they wanted to know. I told them.

'A magnificent house,' said Jean-Jacques, suddenly interested. 'Did you notice the entablatures?'

Actually I had not.

'Look at them properly next time. Friezes of grapes and ravens carved in stone, Corinthian capitals under the parapet... A grand residence. Of course the interior has been spoilt beyond recovery. Offices... Offices and flats. It had a name once. It was called the Hôtel des Corbeaux, on account of the carvings. It was built, if I remember rightly, towards the end of the sixteen-sixties. An eighteenth-century philosopher whose name I can't remember used to live there at one time.'

'During the eighteenth century, I suppose,' said Marianne quietly, and moved up several notches in my estimation. I had been impressed last night by the way she did her job, remaining calm even in the face of the most obstreperous customers, fulfilling the dual role of barmaid and waitress throughout the busiest time of the evening. I'd thought her graceful and attractive. Now I decided she was fun as well. I noticed that her wedding finger was ring-less.

I asked if it was possible to have just one course, a steak for instance, and a carafe of wine. It was and so, after returning the compliment of Jean-Jacques's kir (*Je mange pas*, the poet had said again in reply to my polite mumbles about eating) I squeezed myself into a seat. Not at the big table tonight but at a very small one in a line of four, each of which was squashed so tightly up against its neighbours that only the fact that each wobbled separately indicated its independence from them. On either side of me two couples faced each other, both wrapped up in their own private conversations which were delivered at normal volume, each pair oblivious of their neighbours despite the elbow to elbow proximity. At least the seat opposite me was empty, which created a little space. Now Marianne brought my meal. But someone was making towards the empty seat. It was Dominique, red-scarfed and eager-eyed. He sat down. 'Good news,' he said, adding when I looked blankly at him, 'Your moving in.' I offered him a glass of wine from my carafe. Dominique did not say no.

'You're going to live in the Hôtel des Corbeaux.'

'News travels fast,' I said.

'Luisa told me. Your concierge. That's what concierges are for.' He leaned across towards me, conspirator fashion. 'But it's a house full of history, the Corbeaux.' Dominique seemed even more of a *corbeau* himself this evening: all beak, black plumage and sharp eyes.

'I know. Jean-Jacques told me.'

'Not his sort of history.' Dominique gave a delighted chuckle, something between a wheeze and a croak. 'I mean my sort of history. In the time of the old concierge, when a concierge was a real concierge...'

I wasn't too sure if I would like Dominique's kind of history. 'Yes,' I interrupted. 'What happened to all the old dragons?'

'They died as all dragons do. These days the job is done by Portuguese women whose husbands work in the building trade. It's very useful when it comes to getting jobs done around the house or finding an odd length of copper piping for example. And, by the way, we're not supposed to call them concierges any more; they're *gardiennes*. The money never was very good and it isn't now. Instead they've upped the title. *Comme toujours*... Now this old concierge was a bit deaf but she had a granddaughter, a real looker, who used to visit her during the holidays. That was when I was about sixteen. My God, that girl was something. Used to have a *chambre de bonne* under the roof. Top bell on the left...'

'My bell,' I blurted out, then wished I hadn't. I wasn't especially pleased by the coincidence. 'But I think I've got two *chambres de bonnes* that have been knocked through to make a studio.'

'Right,' said Dominique. 'It's been modernised since those days. And I hope for your sake they've put a new bed in.' He chuckled again, even more throatily. 'Saw some action, the old one. Thank God for electronic entry codes, the push buttons. In the old days it would have been impossible to get in. You used to have to bawl your own name if you got home after midnight to get the concierge to come and open up. Can you imagine? No chance in the old days. I mean, suppose you said you'd come to screw their granddaughter? I give you a toast to the electronic door code.' He helped himself to another glass of wine.

'Also, there was a suicide attempt there about the same time. One of Madame d'Alabouvette's daughters. Of course Margueritte herself won't tell you that. She'll say it was an accident.'

I didn't imagine that she would say anything to me on the subject at all. But I found I was enjoying Dominique's company in spite of myself. I thought my contact with him, like my contacts with Joe and with Fabrice, might help me to become more rapidly a part of the neighbourhood. So when the steak and wine were at an end and Dominique suggested a visit to the Little Horseshoe, *le Petit Fer à Cheval*, I did not protest. 'Why not?' I said. I told him I'd gone there last night with Fabrice.

I paid my bill on the way out. Marianne would accept money for the steak only. 'There won't be any charge for the wine. Dominique drank most of it.'

'I don't think restaurants do that in England,' I said.

'C'est dommage,' said Marianne. What a shame.

*

'You have a friendly face,' said Dominique. Such was the crush at the counter that it was only inches from my own. 'I'll give you a piece of free advice. That woman you sat next to at dinner last night, Françoise, in the yellow dress. You could have her if you wanted. Quite easily. She'll go with anyone.'

I said, 'Thank you for the compliment.'

'You know that's not what I meant. And she's not without funds either. Owns her own shop.'

'Yes,' I said. 'She told me that. But, though I'm grateful for the...' I struggled to remember the word I'd learned for a tip. 'For the *tuyau*, I don't think really that she's what I'm looking for.'

'What are you looking for exactly?' Dominique looked

searchingly into my eyes as if he expected to find the answer there rather than in anything I might say.

I guessed this was a tactic that Dominique used frequently; also that, whatever anyone might divulge by way of a reply Dominique would probably promise to supply it. 'To tell the truth,' I said, 'I don't think I really know at the moment.' It seemed the safest answer.

But Dominique was well prepared for even that. 'You should decide soon, in that case,' he said. 'Life is a full bath with the plug already out when you get in it.'

FIVE

Paris. Winter. 1987.

The room was willing me to get up. Moving only my eyes, I surveyed it. I lay in a bed that would disappear, as soon as I was out of it, into a niche in a clever arrangement of cupboards and bookcases. In the middle of the floor was a coffee table. There were two easy chairs. Under the window was a good-sized desk, the morning sun now falling full upon it, which doubled as my dining table. There were two dining chairs. The outside wall sloped inwards – gently from floor to window height, more steeply above – on account of the mansard roof. Posters would be a possibility there but pictures in frames were out. The floor carpet had a jazzy pattern that wouldn't have been my choice, although I admitted that it was at least cheerful. Out of sight was a very small kitchen and next to it an even smaller bathroom. It was the kind of apartment that estate agents flatter with the word compact. I was pleased with the place. It would do.

From the skylight in my bathroom I had a view (provided I stood on the lavatory seat and held the window open to its fullest extent with an upraised arm) of the spire of Notre Dame. This morning being Sunday the bells in the west towers, which were sadly hidden by an intervening satellite dish, were in full cry, heard by the faithful and the faithless alike as they cowered in their bolt-holes or scurried on their own pursuits about the city.

I was not a religious person: an Anglican by default, I had rarely attended a church service in adult life. But I did believe – hope triumphing over experience? – in the power of human love and was attracted to the idea that there might be a more profound reality behind this love: a reserve of solid gold that underpinned the ephemeral currency exchanged by humankind. Whatever the reason, spiritual, nostalgic or touristic, I decided this morning, listening to the bells, that I would go to Notre Dame and hear Mass.

The air was still and sharp and a mist lay lightly over the Seine, binding together the Ile de la Cité and the Ile de St Louis just above the waterline like a silken web. Before the cathedral's west front a large crowd was gathered despite the cold: tourists and worshippers whisked together in an emulsion, like oil and vinegar for vinaigrette.

The clammy shock of the darkness inside separated the emulsion out. Worshippers were passing through a narrow gate under the scrutiny of a warden who with a well chosen question barred the way of non-worshippers and the ill-dressed and cast them into the outer darkness of the side aisles: tourists in countless swarms like lost souls. These produced an unchanging, shuffling sound of unrest: the sound perhaps of wailing and teeth-gnashing heard at a great distance. I decided to try and join the worshippers in the nave and was slightly surprised to be let in unchallenged, as if winning a competition I had not entered.

Above the high altar hung a coronet of lights through which the smoke of incense billowed up at intervals and, beyond, lances of blue stained glasslight pried their way between the soaring columns of the apse. The Mass was sung in Latin, the multinational congregation of thousands joining in the chants, and when so many voices were raised in different timbres and accents to sing the Pater Noster, I, for whom the situation was without precedent in my insular experience of churchgoing, was surprised by an emotion that caught at my throat and pricked behind my eyes.

Afterwards, when I shuffled out of the gloom of incense and blue glasslight, a survival instinct that had been sharpening with every day of my new life suggested that coffee and croissants on the terraces immediately around the cathedral would cost more than my status as a resident warranted. I crossed the bridge back into the Marais and went to look for a café that was open, a search that brought me quickly to the Little Horseshoe where, despite the chill, I installed myself at one of the pavement tables that were set out in optimistic response to the morning sun.

I guessed as I waited for my croissants to appear that if I only sat there long enough the whole population of the Marais would pass before my eyes. I'd also have been prepared to bet that Dominique would be the first.

I was wrong. The first comer was Fabrice. I was surprised to see Fabrice without his girlfriend. With a gesture I invited Fabrice to join me at my table. 'I almost didn't see you,' he said. At that moment my croissants arrived.

Fabrice ordered a coffee then watched me devour the croissants with rapt attention, as if he were going to paint the scene. 'You look as if you haven't eaten for days,' he said.

'I've been to Mass,' I said.

I told the story of my meeting with Margueritte and its satisfactory outcome, making appropriate thanking noises for Fabrice's part in making it happen. I asked after Régine. With an upward flick of his eyes Fabrice told me she'd had to go to Bordeaux for the weekend: a family problem, a grandmother breaking a leg or something. Why it had to involve Régine he could not imagine but there it was. So he was alone for the weekend. With a house stocked with food. Would I like to come to his flat for lunch? The invitation had virtually made itself. I accepted.

There was something very compelling about Fabrice. He had a warmth that was highly comforting. He seemed almost without edges and I welcomed that.

For what was left of the morning we observed the life of the *quartier* as it passed before us. There was a man who wore a live white rat around his shoulder nonchalantly as if it were a scarf; a woman who carried a dog, not much larger than the rat, in her shopping bag wherever she went; she walked with an alarming limp – alarming for the dog, that was; it rose and fell through a sixty-degree arc at each lurching step, wearing the intent

The Paris Novel

expression of a yachtsman negotiating a choppy sea. At one point a tiny, shrill-voiced man accosted Fabrice, railing against a neighbour of his: a monster, a devil incarnate, a Spaniard called Carlos. Later came a mild and gentle Spaniard, equally diminutive, who complained of his neighbour, a bully and a thief, a Portuguese named Nico. 'Nico was the first one,' explained Fabrice, when Carlos had gone.

'How did I guess?' I said.

'They're two of the concierges round here,' Fabrice explained. 'Rarely if ever seen together. *Les deux ouistitis* we call them, the two marmosets.'

Fabrice told me a little of the Marais's chequered history. A swampy area of slums before Henri IV built his palace there – now the place des Vosges – it had then become the most fashionable part of the city. The house I lived in dated from this time. Later the Marais had declined with the removal of the court to Versailles and then the revolution till, within recent memory, it was a slum again, quaintly awful for the tourists, grim and insanitary for its population. 'They were going to pull it down, it was all so rotten. Luckily they didn't. Look at it now. And it's one of the few bits of Paris that Baron Haussman never got his hands on. Virtually untouched by the nineteenth century.'

We had left the café by now and were on the way to Fabrice's apartment. We stopped at a corner shop to collect baguettes and other last-minute items. I bought a suitably generous bottle of wine. The shop was run by a

Moroccan woman, Fabrice said. A Madame Almuslih. Plus her two children. Between them they kept the shop stocked and selling from dawn to dusk six days a week and from dawn to lunchtime on Sundays. 'Her husband is in prison of course,' said Fabrice casually as we left the shop. 'That's why she works so hard.'

'In prison for what?' asked Peter.

'Murder, I think,' said Fabrice. 'No-one's sure exactly. One can't really ask her.'

'I suppose not.'

'The locksmith over the road is in prison too,' Fabrice went on. 'Quite funny actually. He made copies of all his clients' keys and burgled them when they were out. It wasn't till he started driving around in a Porsche that people began to get suspicious.'

Compared to mine, Fabrice's flat appeared a palace. I'd only glimpsed it briefly and drunkenly on my first visit. I had just seen the living-room spin round once before I collapsed into sleep and I hadn't stayed for breakfast the following morning. 'Don't be too impressed,' Fabrice said, though his tone was not over-modest. 'The bank pays for it all. They sent me over from Strasbourg so they pay. It's officially for one but there's room for Régine and the bank hasn't made any problems.'

The principal room –*le living*, Fabrice called it – had a fine parquet floor covered with oriental rugs while a gilt-framed mirror occupied the whole of the wall space above a carved marble fireplace. The walls themselves were panelled, painted white, and a modest chandelier twinkled benevolently beneath a moulded plaster ceiling. *'Quand-même,'* I said. I was beginning to get the hang of that word. It meant something like *even so*. In this instance it meant that, whoever paid for the apartment, I was impressed anyway.

Fabrice poured an aperitif and suggested that we drink it in the kitchen while he prepared lunch. In any case the kitchen was the dining-room as well. We continued to talk as Fabrice cooked, over glasses of Pineau de Charentes, which Fabrice twice refilled.

'Why did you come to Paris?' Fabrice asked inevitably at one point. This looked like the beginning of the conversation Fabrice had wanted two nights ago but which we hadn't got round to.

I shrugged. 'New start, I suppose. Wanting to be a writer... I split with my girlfriend recently. Usual story. You've heard it a thousand times.'

Fabrice nodded gravely. 'Yeah. I know.' Actually he said it in French. *'Ouais, je sais.'* He was paying my own French a compliment by speaking it.

Fabrice's competence in the kitchen was of a pretty high order, I thought. Joints of rabbit appeared from somewhere, had themselves coated in Dijon mustard, were popped into an oven dish, received great bastings of cream and butter and then left to their own devices in the oven. Salads were prepared, cheeses were sniffed for something (ripeness? off-flavours?) and either chosen or rejected. Herbs were chopped, the fruit bowl's contents deftly transformed into a fruit salad with the addition of something alcoholic and aromatic from a bottle, two-tone pasta selected and put to boil... Even if Fabrice was not a three-star chef or his results in the same class as Maxim's, I knew that, had it been me unexpectedly entertaining a near stranger to Sunday lunch, it would not have been like this.

'And Régine? Does she cook too?' I asked.

'No, not really. She has a repertoire of great dishes which she does very well but she's not an everyday cook at all. I do that. On the other hand, she mixes excellent cocktails and she chooses the wine.'

'Sounds a perfect partnership.' I was glad I'd brought a good bottle to accompany the meal. Without it Fabrice's lavish hospitality might have been overwhelming.

Fabrice told me about his family home in Alsace, near the town of Saverne. He did so in a very matter-of-fact way without any trace of boastfulness or desire to impress but it was clear from his description that he had been born rather luckier than most. His father, just coming up to retirement, was in investment banking as Fabrice was himself, and he owned a fairly stately pile on the edge of one of those half-timbered, geranium-sprouting Alsace villages that make the tourists go all misty eyed. There was an estate with tenant farmers, gamekeepers and the lot. Did I shoot? I never had done, but quickly – oh how quickly – I added that this was for no other reason than lack of opportunity. An invitation seemed to be looming in the vinous lunchtime haze, and even before it was made I watched my egalitarian principles vanish into the mist along with all the ties I felt with the extremely modest edge-of-town house in Northampton where my parents still lived and where my father, stern and principled, gave up his spare time to sit on the hard benches of the council chamber as a Labour representative.

'You must come for a weekend sometime very soon – and I mean very soon, because the shooting season's almost up. Say next weekend. What about it?' The invitation had come swiftly and, just as swiftly, I said I'd love to come.

With after-lunch coffee came a large glass of Armagnac and with that, the realisation that I would have to abandon my plans for the afternoon. I'd meant to finish settling into the flat, tidy odds and ends, sort papers. That would all have to be postponed now until after a siesta. After the Armagnac it seemed that the moment had come for me to leave. I remembered the washing up and offered to do it, but Fabrice would not hear of it. He quite understood that I had things to do; moving was such a headache. He pointed out the bedroom as we passed it on the way to the door: another magnificent room complete with enormous mirror and chandelier. I said thank you for the lunch and we shook hands. 'I'm beginning to get used to shaking everybody's hand twice a day,' I said. 'It's a bit of a novelty for us English.'

'Yes,' Fabrice agreed. 'You don't enjoy physical

contact the way we do.'

I laughed. 'I don't accept that. You'd change your mind if you got to know us a little better.'

'I'd like very much to do that,' said Fabrice, at the same moment turning the wish to deed with a sudden enveloping embrace whose meaning, since we were in a bedroom, was unambiguous even to someone as clueless as me. Fabrice was the bigger and easily the stronger of us and a second later I found myself struggling on my back on the rather sumptuous silk coverlet with which the double bed was draped, with Fabrice on top of me and kissing me enthusiastically while, with the one hand that was sandwiched between our two bodies, trying to undo my zip. For several seconds I struggled with arms and legs to free myself, though vocal protest was more or less impossible. Fortunately Fabrice had both the sense and the good manners to let me go as soon as he realised that no amount of persistence would kindle any kind of reciprocal lust in me. He stood up off the bed and ran a hand through his hair as if running up a flag of truce. But he didn't look in the least embarrassed or apologetic.

I bobbed up into a standing position too. For a split second I thought I was going to hit Fabrice but the feeling passed off surprisingly quickly. Bizarrely I found myself concentrating on the sensation of Fabrice's kissing me. It was the first time my own moustached upper lip had ever brushed against another one that was similarly adorned. It had felt surprisingly … well, different. I was astonished, the next moment, to hear myself coming out with the French equivalent of 'Well, now I really must he going,' quite calmly though a little breathlessly. *'Bon, il faut qui je m'en aille. Au revoir.'*

'Au revoir,' said Fabrice. He sounded a little disappointed but not at all angry or ashamed. Then to my further surprise – though not much further surprise was now possible – he added in effortless English, 'Oh don't be so British, Peter. I can't help it. You're just so cute.' He smiled down at me from the landing as I stumbled down the stairs.

SIX

'And were you 'shocking', as my students love to say?' Joe asked. We were sitting outside the café he had taken me to two days ago. There was an amused twinkle in his eyes. 'The French believe that the English are always 'shocking' by anything overtly sexual. The preconception and the grammar mistake are ingrained together. But really, were you shocking?'

'Shocked, no. Surprised? Well, yes, I was a little. I mean it didn't seem to grow out of anything. It was a touch unexpected.'

'Do you want to rephrase the last sentence? No, but I like the sound of your Sunday. High Mass at Notre Dame in the morning and a proposition from an investment banker under the chandelier in the afternoon. You seem to live life with an inbuilt sense of style.' He broke off. 'Or do you? No, I'm quite wrong. It's rather that things happen to you with style. Are you one of those people who never seek adventure but to whom adventures simply happen? What's that other word? Befall, that's it. Befall, befell, befallen. You're a befallen man, Peter. You should be careful.'

'What do you mean?'

'I don't know,' said Joe, with a self-deprecating smile. 'How the hell should I know what I mean? Oh but yes, I do know. Some people don't create their own lives: they're always on the receiving end of them. Watch out that you don't become one of those or the whole of life will happen to you without you doing anything to it. It'll be over and there you'll be, all befallen.'

'Anyway,' I tried to reassert myself, 'the point is, what do I say to him next time we meet? I can't exactly cut him dead. We live almost next door, we use the same cafés and restaurants, know the same people... I'd actually accepted an invitation to go to Alsace with him next weekend.'

'I don't see what you're so wound up about.'

'I'm not wound up.'

'You are, or you wouldn't have mentioned it. Despite your air of apparent calm, your English phlegm, you are wound up. But I don't get why you think you need to react in some way. You don't have to do anything, or say anything, or even think about it; it's no big deal. Treat him like nothing happened. He won't refer to it or try it again. Or if he does, just tell him to go to hell if that's how you feel about it. And if you don't want to spend a weekend in the country with him just tell him something else has cropped up. Nothing could be less complicated. But for God's sake don't go round trying to avoid him. That's just inconvenient and a good way to make both of you paranoid.' He reflected a half second. 'All the same, it might be prudent not to get drunk together in his bedroom again.'

'Thanks,' I said. 'I'll try to bear the last point in mind. But seriously, what's he doing with a girlfriend if he's like that? And if he isn't, what was he doing yesterday?'

'Well, he might be bisexual. But much more likely, he's just a normal, healthy, fun-loving frog. Why do you want to know, anyway?' Joe grinned wickedly. 'Interested after all?'

'Bollocks. Or bullshit if you prefer. I just haven't had much to do with gay people. I don't know how they tick. Perhaps I've led a sheltered life.'

I was joking when I said that, but Joe didn't seem to realise that. 'Now *that's* bullshit,' he said. 'Nobody leads a sheltered life these days. It's you, trying to be conventional and seeing only what's conventional around you. Of course you have contact with gay people; that's a matter of statistics. And anyway, here you are, having a drink with me. Or hadn't you even realised that?'

'I suppose I had. Had an inkling, anyway.'

'An inkling? You know, I was going to ask you to dinner later in the week, *chez moi*. Guess that won't be so easy now. If you're going to be afraid every other male in Paris is trying to make you...'

He broke off, peered at his glass, turned it a hundred and eighty degrees and then addressed it. 'What can we poor babies do? Let a straight guy think we fancy him and he runs one point six one kilometres. Let him know we don't and he never forgives us for it.'

I said, 'I think I can understand that. O.K. I tell you

what. If I promise not to think about either possibility, perhaps you could pay me the compliment of doing the same.'

'Yeah, but I couldn't, you see,' said Joe with a twist of his head. 'You may be able to ignore it but I never can. I'm built that way.'

'Then maybe you could pretend to ignore it,' I suggested. 'At least when you're with me. Would that be possible, for the sake of ... friendship?'

Joe gave his glass another half turn. 'For the sake of friendship,' he said slowly, 'I might just manage that.'

I thought of asking Joe if he wanted to eat with me at the Figeac. I wanted him to meet Fabrice. And Régine? I tried to imagine the scene but the picture would not come. Another time, perhaps. And yet...

A flick of one switch in heart or brain would bring to my lips the formula, 'What are you doing this evening?' A flick of another and my eyes would twitch towards my watch while the words came, 'It's time I was going.' The latter occurred. For what reason? A look crossing Joe's face, registered only unconsciously by me? Pressure building in my bladder that I was hardly aware of? From such trivial causes hurricanes are said to spring. But for now there was no hurricane. 'It's time I was going,' I said, and I got up. Later I went by myself to the Figeac and Joe went off on his own to get a baguette from his local boulangerie.

*

The house I lived in really was very beautiful, as Jean-Jacques had said. I made a point of looking at the entablatures of carved ravens and grapes when I went back there that night. Walking through the carriage doors into the central courtyard I could harmlessly pretend that it all belonged to me and that I took the back stairs in preference to the lift for the sake of the exercise. Luisa had been helpful over the last two days, despite a little language difficulty: my accent was strange to her while her French had a disconcerting tendency to wander into Portuguese and back again in the space of a few words. Still, she had always got through in the end, telling me where to shop, offering spare light-bulbs, recommending a launderette. As for the various sons and daughters of Margueritte, contact had been limited to exchanged *bonjours* in the courtyard; they recognising me by my accent, I them by their prominent, high-born lips. Of Monsieur Guyot, whoever he might be, there was no sign. Although it was late, I sat at my little table and wrote.

Paris. Winter. 1987.

The baguette worn under the arm is one of the supreme clichés of Parisian life and as such it is a badge of belonging that no self-respecting foreign resident can be without. Every street corner has its boulangerie and every Parisian too, each certain that his or her preferred bread shop is better than all the others. Madame Dumont, for example, lives at the top of the rue des Archives but swears by the baker at the bottom. Monsieur Dupont, on the other hand, lives at the bottom but favours the bakery at the top. They pass each other in the street twice each day like two sentries on duty, and nod and say bonjour, each carrying like a rifle what they firmly hold to be the best baguette in Paris.

*

I unlaced a shoe. After a moment it fell of its own accord. I was unsure onto whose ceiling. Monsieur Guyot's perhaps. I'd dined relatively soberly at the Figeac with Dominique and Françoise, a little relieved that Fabrice and Régine had not been there. I felt that Sunday needed a few days to get over, especially if I decided to take Joe's advice and forget the whole episode. Perhaps Fabrice thought so too.

Françoise had been on good social form, chirruping like one of Madame Touret's canaries, a resemblance heightened by the deep orange meringue of a dress she was wearing as if in an attempt to turn early March to high summer. I guessed she used her shop as a vast personal wardrobe from which to select creations to suit her every mood or invitation. She missed the sun more with each passing winter, she told me, and, *à propos*, a man to take her to it. She looked quite directly at me while she said this. People seemed to do that a lot here. Warmer climates suited her temperament, she said. In them she blossomed. I had exchanged a glance with Dominique.

I unlaced the other shoe and let it fall to join its partner on the floor. Then I got up and loaded a tape into my cassette player.

Every traveller was in those days a desert island castaway where music was concerned because of the logistics of luggage. I had with me only a slender library of cassette tapes, a selection I'd chosen with as much rigour as any guest invited on the radio programme. Tonight I chose Beethoven, a choice that would have surprised the younger me: I was a recent convert. I picked out the performance of the Waldstein piano sonata that had been recorded by Artur Schnabel in the nineteen-thirties. It was the recording against which, I'd read or someone had told me, all subsequent ones had to stand or fall.

It was a brilliant, diamantine piece, sculpted with almost Mozartean precision. Contemporary critics had described it as glacial; Wagner had even nicknamed it the Dispassionata. But with repeated listening I'd learned better. Beethoven had set springs of passion beneath the frozen surface that would explode beneath your feet and sweep you away on a cascading torrent... But only when you the listener, you the person, were ready.

After that I continued to write...

*

The music ended and silence and darkness filled the flat. I walked to the window and looked out. The mansards of the building opposite stood sightless but above them, on a higher level than my own, an upper attic signalled its existence by a solitary dormer that seemed to be peering skywards, casting its warm light up. It had the beckoning quality that had so struck me on my first night in the capital. So small this light was, yet so generous with its meagre resources that it seemed to want to turn night into day, so optimistically did it pour itself into the blue dark.

*

I looked up from my notebook and watched that lit attic window for several more minutes, uncertain of the feelings the sight evoked in me, before I pulled the shutters to and went to bed.

Anthony McDonald

SEVEN

I became aware of a banging sound. It crescendoed up through my sleep, dragging me into an unwilling consciousness.

I sat up in bed and switched on the light. It revealed my Paris studio, quite unchanged since I'd gone to bed in it. I glanced at my watch, which said three o'clock, and tried to come to terms with the fact that there was someone outside the door just six feet away who very much wanted to be on the inside. Because of the entry code lock on the street door the caller had to be, in theory at least, one of my neighbours: a d'Alabouvettes or perhaps the mysterious Monsieur Guyot. But why would they disturb me at such an hour? Fire? I got up and moved towards the door, calling loudly, 'Who is it?' in English before remembering that French would be more appropriate.

The knocking ceased as soon as I spoke and a voice said, *'C'est moi: Dominique.'*

I stopped in my tracks and did not undo the door. 'What do you want?' I said.

'I want to come in,' said the voice. It sounded more than agitated but it was unmistakeably Dominique's. 'I've killed my wife.'

For some reason I felt reassured by this announcement. I knew that Dominique didn't have a wife. Therefore he could not have killed her. Therefore it was safe to let him in. The possibility that I was opening the door to a lunatic at three in the morning did not present itself. It was only when Dominique stood in the room with me, fully dressed in outdoor clothes, a suddenly important two inches taller than I was that I, in bare feet and a bath robe, began to feel a bit vulnerable. 'Sit down,' I said at once in an effort to improve things by a change of eye-line. Dominique did as he was told; I stayed standing.

For someone who had not recently killed his wife Dominique managed an impressive performance as someone who had. He shook uncontrollably and his hands, which seemed to have taken on lives of their own, wandered variously over his face, his body and the armchair on which he perched rather than sat. His mouth worked as if trying sentences that would not come. My experience of real murderers was non-existent. But I did know that drunks might also behave like this.

'Tell me about it,' I said. 'How did it happen?'

'At the Figeac.' Dominique spoke quietly, haltingly. 'She refused to come home with me. I lost my rag. She dug in. I grabbed her, pulled her towards me. She began to shout. Somehow we were in the kitchen. I got hold of a knife. I didn't know what I was doing...' He burst into a fit of sobs and covered his face with his hands.

I sat down opposite him, unsure what to do or say. I pressed the tips of my fingers together like an actor playing a detective, leaned forward and said, 'She. Who do you mean by she? Who is your wife?'

'Marianne,' he said. Bloody hell, I thought.

'Are you sure she's dead?' I asked him. 'Not just hurt?'

Dominique's head jerked up and he gave me a look of pathetic intensity. 'You think perhaps she's not dead then?'

'Did you see her after you touched her?'

'No. I ran out of the kitchen. I left the restaurant. I heard her screaming but I ran.'

'When did this happen?'

'Fifteen minutes ago. I'm sure she's dead.'

'You can't be sure,' I said. I willed Marianne not to be dead. Then I said, 'Why did you come here? Why to me? You hardly know me. How did you get in?'

But even as I was speaking I remembered that, as a teenager, Dominique had had a fling with a girl who lived in this very room. He knew the door code. Ancient memories, associations of comfort and reassurance, might easily have sent him flying up here in a blind or drunken panic.

Dominique said, 'I went to Fabrice first. Looking for you both.' Looking for us both?! At Fabrice's flat? That gave me an almighty jolt. Dominique went on. 'There was no answer. I came here then.' He added, *'J'ai confiance en toi.'* I trust you.

There was silence. At last I broke it. 'What do you want me to do?'

'Don't know.'

'I think,' I said, trying to do just that, 'that we need first to discover if Marianne is really dead. If we went together to the Figeac, perhaps?'

Dominique shook his head vigorously.

'Then, if I went alone?'

This seemed to please him better. But he grabbed my arm and said, 'You won't go to the police? Promise. You mustn't. Say you haven't seen me. I'll be waiting for you here.'

I had the sinking feeling of someone who has woken up, not out of a nightmare but into one. I saw myself leaving my studio at the mercy of a maniac who might, for all I knew, be a thief into the bargain; I'd return to find my few valuables gone. Or just possibly Dominique was telling the truth; then I'd be charged with harbouring a murderer, I'd come under who knew what suspicion... and all in French. I considered telling Dominique to get out of the flat, locking the door against him, washing my hands of the whole matter. But would Dominique go quietly if I asked him to? Dominique was not a giant but I had no illusions about who would win if it came to a struggle. I was suddenly acutely conscious of my kitchen drawer, of the fact that it was nearer to me than to Dominique, and of the exact position of all the utensils in it. But some instinct told me that Dominique would in fact go quietly. There would be no ugly or dangerous scene; only Dominique would be hurt, let down, almost literally, like someone who jumps into a safety blanket only to see it withdrawn. And Dominique had said, *'J'ai confiance en toi.'*

'I promise,' I said, and heard a sigh in my voice. 'I won't say where you are if it's humanly possible not to. *J'ai confiance en toi, moi aussi.*' I made my way towards the door.

Dominique was watching me. 'You'd better put some clothes on,' he said flatly.

*

I let myself out into the dark street. Someone was running towards me. He passed beneath a street-lamp. It was Fabrice. I'd never been more pleased to see anyone in my life. I nearly wept with relief.

'Where is he?' Fabrice asked.

'Upstairs in my flat,' I said. Somehow I'd got hold of Fabrice's hands and was clasping them.

'Are you all right?' Fabrice asked earnestly, I felt his hands shake with his concern for me.

'Yes. Why? Is he dangerous? He says he's killed Marianne. At the Figeac.'

'Merde,' said Fabrice. 'We'd better get over there.'

'I was on my way,' I said.

As we neared the corner that would bring us in sight of the restaurant I steeled myself in readiness for the two possible scenes that would greet us: the blaze of lights and swarms of police cars that would indicate that Dominique's story was true, or the quiet, untroubled, three-in-the-morning darkness that would mean it was not. Neither possibility gave me much comfort. We rounded the corner.

The Figeac was a blaze of lights. People were clustered on the pavement round an ambulance whose doors were being shut. It drove off as we arrived. There were no police cars.

'Where's Dominique?' Madame Touret demanded almost before **we** reached the group on the pavement. Her face was set in an expression I'd not known it capable of till now, the corners of her mouth turned firmly down.

But I was not ready to abandon my promise just yet. 'Tell me what happened to Marianne,' I said. 'Is she dead? Injured? What?' The question of whether she was or was not Dominique's wife could wait.

'Is that what Dominique sent you to find out?' Madame Touret's tone was scornful. She looked from me to Fabrice then back again. She said a little more gently, 'She isn't dead. She isn't dead and she isn't in danger. You'll be able to tell Dominique that.'

We were inside the restaurant now: Fabrice and I, Madame Touret, her son and chef René, and Jean-

Jacques with copy of *Libération* still in pocket though by now it was yesterday's. Presumably it would only be jettisoned in order to make way for the new one. René offered everyone a brandy. Even Jean-Jacques' liver raised no objection. The police had not been called, it was explained. Everyone had agreed that it was a purely domestic matter.

'But is she his wife?' I asked Fabrice.

'No,' he answered. 'At least, I don't think so.'

'You are correct,' Jean-Jacques told him. 'She lives with another man, quite happily as far as I know, in the *Cinquième*.'

'Dominique has a lot of imagination,' said Madame Touret. A slightly hooded look crossed her face.

'But what was tonight about?' Fabrice asked. 'That wasn't imagination. Marianne's injured.'

Madame Touret touched his forearm gently. 'Not injured badly, though she's in shock, hence the ambulance. He wouldn't really hurt someone. The knife scratched her, not much more. If he thinks he did more damage than that, then it is a *folie de grandeur*.'

'Or guilt,' suggested Jean-Jacques.

Madame Touret ignored him and continued to speak to Fabrice and me. 'Whatever impression you may have got tonight, he isn't violent. You don't have to worry about that. He has a good heart.'

The Paris Novel

'Good but crazy,' said her son the chef.

'I won't let you say that,' objected Madame. She turned back to Fabrice and me. 'He has some problems which lead him to weave fantasies about himself and about other people. I've known him since he was a child. Believe me, I understand him. A few months ago he got it into his head that Marianne was going to be his girlfriend, perhaps his wife. It was harmless at first. Just a joke. Later it became more serious. He pestered her at closing time, though he knew she lived with someone else. Tonight he became impossible. The fantasy took over. He seemed to think he was married to her already.'

'Problems?' Jean-Jacques said. 'He's a drunk, and drugged with I don't know what cocktails of *merde*. That's his problem if he has one. He needs medical help. Professional treatment. Counselling.'

'Don't talk nonsense.' Madame Touret rounded on him sharply. 'He needs a good woman to love him, that's all. Nothing more complicated than that.'

'He's hardly going the best way about finding one,' I said, and was shocked to hear myself, a newcomer and a foreigner, throwing my tuppence-worth into what was, I began to suspect, a family argument.

'I assure you,' Madame Touret told me – also a bit sharply, 'he is perfectly harmless.'

'It's good to hear that,' Fabrice said. 'You see, he's in Peter's flat right now. We're not quite sure how to deal with him.'

Madame gave us a look I shall never forget. 'Oh, don't be so wet, the pair of you. You must talk to him. Get him to go home.'

I felt a sudden urge to be supportive of Fabrice. We kept being bracketed together this evening. Well, we would stand or fall together then. 'Us?' I said. 'He's hardly our problem. And what are we supposed to say to him? One person says he needs professional help, another that he needs a woman. Then you throw him at us. I don't even know him!'

'It's not exactly we who are throwing him at you,' Jean-Jacques objected. 'He appears to have done that himself. Though why he should have chosen your place to run to rather than to anyone else's in the neighbourhood I don't know. You must have made some sort of impression.'

You obviously don't know about the old concierge's grand-daughter, I thought. I said, 'He said he trusted me.' I added, I wasn't sure why, 'He trusted us.'

'Then you must talk to him as best you can,' said Jean-Jacques calmly. 'I'm only a poet, not an oracle. But if you want one piece of advice, let it be this: it isn't the words you will use that matter – it's not what you'll say but the fact that you say it. Now *bon courage*.'

Fabrice and I had been dismissed. Together we left the restaurant.

We walked back to my place together. We didn't say much. There is something very companionable about walking side by side along a street with a friend when you have a common purpose. I'd realised that when we were walking up the rue Vieille du Temple a few nights back. The more so on the return walk, when our common concern had been to stop each other falling over.

And then there I was, showing my merchant banker friend into my small and unimpressive studio at three in the morning. Into a flat where a drunken nutter awaited us. Perhaps.

Dominique was still there. He was now sitting on my bed, elbows on knees and head in hands. We would never know whether he'd sat all the time like that, or whether he'd adopted the pose when he heard us climbing the stairs.

We hadn't planned any kind of strategy, Fabrice and I. It just happened the way it did. Fabrice went and sat on the bed on one side of Dominique and I sat down the other side of him.

'It's all OK,' I heard Fabrice say. His head was hidden from my sight by Dominique's.

'Marianne's unhurt,' I said, picking up where Fabrice had left off. 'She's in hospital but only for shock.'

'What do I do next?' Dominique asked. He seemed genuinely lost.

'A notre avis...' I heard Fabrice say. *We think...* I can't easily describe the effect that unexpected plural had on

me. It filled me with complex thoughts at a moment when everything already seemed complex enough. I had to focus carefully in order to hear how Fabrice would complete the thought. I heard him say, 'We think you should go home now. In the morning early, go to the hospital and take her flowers.'

For some reason the sheer banality of what Fabrice was saying on behalf of both of us brought a lump to my throat. I heard myself say, 'He's right, Dominique. Just do that.'

And then Dominique stood up, thanked us both, and left. It was as weirdly simple as that. I felt the way you do when you try to unpick a knot or something, and think it'll never sort itself, and then suddenly it does.

And that left me and Fabrice sitting next to each other on my small bed. I remembered Joe's words: *It might be prudent not to get drunk together in his bedroom again.* Or in mine. I stood up. 'I guess it's time we said goodnight,' I said. So then Fabrice stood up.

I walked down the stairs with him. We didn't touch. Then, as I opened the postern gate in the big courtyard door I found that we'd embraced. I held him, and he held me, for a second or two, and then he leaned in towards me, inclined his head – he was the taller one – and kissed me on the cheek.

'Oh hey,' I said, in mild protest. We unhooked ourselves and said goodnight and I shut the door after he passed through it into the street.

There was something I couldn't understand. On Sunday he'd rolled me onto his bed and smothered me with unwanted kisses. I'd been annoyed by that, though not really upset. But I hadn't felt all that much. It had just been an embarrassing mistake on his part, and perhaps I'd let myself in for it. I'd shrugged it off.

But this time I had felt something. I was a bit shaken by that fact. I didn't think I was happy with it. Even though he hadn't lathered me with kisses this time. It had just been a peck on the cheek. But I had felt something. Though I'd been taken too far out of my comfort zone to know what it was.

Anthony McDonald

EIGHT

Paris. Winter. 1987

I took a walk. It was the end of the first afternoon in March but not cold. Though it was dark. Two days had passed since Fabrice had kissed me on the cheek. I hadn't wanted to see him again. I had wanted to, of course. For both those reasons I had steered clear of the Figeac. I was also steering clear of Marianne and Dominique.

My walk took me down the rue des Archives, across the rue de Rivoli, then down to the quays of the Seine, where the Ile de la Cité appeared in front of me across the water, bristling with beauty and fortresses.

I turned west along the quays. The quai Mégisserie, the quai du Louvre, the quai des Tuileries.

I suppose every gay man comes here in the end.

It seemed as though that long, long wall, the southern wall of the Tuileries gardens that flanked the river, the wall from which no turning led off, had been built for no other reason than that bare-legged, bare-arsed men might fuck each other, standing up against it. Their buttocks were round and smooth and the ambient light ricocheted back from their convex surfaces. The gentle moans that some of them made were palpable in the air. Palpable: it means I felt I could reach out and touch the soft sounds. By extension the soft buttocks, clenched bollocks and hard cocks. I did none of that. I wasn't gay, I told myself.

There was no way out of here. I could go on until I reached the Place de la Concorde after a quarter mile or so, then return by the rue de Rivoli, which ran parallel, the other side of the Tuileries gardens and the Louvre, or turn back at once, and return the way I'd come, reviewing the ranks of naked buttocks in reverse order as I retraced my steps.

I didn't do either of those things exactly. I did walk all the way to the Place de la Concorde, but then I retraced my steps precisely, reviewing the whole half mile of everything as I came back.

*

'People are weird,' said Joe. 'Real weird. What about her boyfriend? You'd think he'd be trying to kill this Dominique character.'

Two more days had passed and this was my first opportunity to talk to Joe. We met at a café on the place Hotel de Ville in the early evening.

I told Joe, 'I heard they met in the hospital corridor. Dominique really did take flowers by the way. Apparently they nodded to each other politely and just passed on without speaking. They won't fight each other.'

Joe shook his head. 'Like I said, people are weird. That includes you, Peter. In fact, especially you. I'm astonished – even shocking – that you let the guy into your room that night in the first place. You run a mile when a merchant banker places his manicured hand on your knee over the petits-fours but you open up to a homicidal maniac at three in the morning. I fail to discern a pattern there. Know what I mean? I'm afraid I'd have told him to fuck off. I really would.' Joe stopped speaking and peered at my chest as if trying to see, in a most literal way, what was at the heart of me.

He looked up again at my face. 'You're an onion,' he said in a conclusive tone of voice. 'Layer beneath layer of you. The question is, though, what is the thread that runs up the centre? The slender translucent fibre that underlies all the layers and that you can easily dissect the onion without finding.'

He changed the subject slightly. 'This book you're writing. Are you writing about all the people you're meeting here? The amorous banker, mad Dominique, me?'

I said, 'I didn't think I was.' There was silence for a moment. We stared out through the plate glass of the café into the square. The fountains played as coldly as ever in the centre of it and the marble gleamed no less glacially under the street lamps. The Hôtel de Ville loomed owl-white to the left of us while straight ahead, beyond the river channel the towers and pinnacles of Notre Dame spear-headed shafts of floodlight into the sky.

'I've fallen in love,' said Joe.

'Really?' I said.

'Oh yes.' Joe mimicked my English accent. 'Really, really, really. Come on. Let's go,' he said.

We paid and walked out into the cold evening air. The fountains continued to play over the white marble and the chill seemed penetrating to the marrow.

'Suddenly? Just like that?' I enquired.

'Too right.'

'I don't believe you,' I told him bluntly. 'Falling in love doesn't happen like that. Or if it does it's not falling in love; it's something else.'

Joe looked at me with mild surprise. 'Bullshit,' he said calmly. 'You're so wrong. At least you are about me. And falling is exactly the right word for it. I've never realized quite how right until now. Fall is exactly what I did. Last Monday night. Just after leaving you. Under a shower of bread and brioche cascading onto the pavement.'

'Please explain,' I said.

So Joe did. Joe had his own favourite boulangerie, just like everyone else. It was halfway between where he got the Métro at Arts et Metier when he went to work and where he lived in the rue Chapon. He'd gone there after we'd parted on Sunday evening.

The relative tranquillity of his short walk was marred by a Sunday night traffic jam and the boulevard was shoulder-high with cars aggressively demanding right of way. He told me it felt as though the traffic was fuelled not by petrol but by a distillation of pure fury under compression. Cars and buses moved in sudden leaps and little dashes, a Morse code of spasmodic progress, halted constantly with shocks to chassis and flashes – sometimes crunches too – of brake lights.

He'd threaded his way through this ill-tempered scrum, slapping hard the backs of those vehicles that showed signs of rolling back – no-one used their mirrors – to crush his legs against the car behind. He'd reached the pavement and the boulangerie. Its door had opened in his face, and out had popped a very young man with a huge openwork basket of long loaves in each hand. They'd had no time to avoid each other. Joe had collided with the boy's left shoulder and his left hand load of bread. The knock had swung the boy round to face Joe but had also made him lose his balance. He staggered, and began to fall.

Joe saw the boy was too afraid of losing the bread he was carrying to grab hold of the door or wall. He'd put out a hand to try to save him, but it had simply made things worse. He ended up shoving at the boy's chest as he fell back but, meeting no resistance, lost his own balance and fell on top of him as he landed on his back.

Falling on top of both of them came a metal trolley and a meteor shower of bread: *baguettes, bâtards, ficelles, pains longs, pains ronds, pains noirs, miches, boules*. French bread in its infinite variety fell pattering on the pavement or flew in all directions in a flurry of flour.

'Merde!' Joe had exclaimed simultaneously with another male voice. Joe found himself looking into a pair of large hazel eyes momentarily frozen like a rabbit's caught in headlights, then suddenly illuminated by a smile. The smile had surprised itself into a laugh. Then Joe had laughed too.

People were picking them up by now, collecting scattered, flattened loaves, asking if anyone was hurt – this last a spontaneous display of public spirit rare in Paris but then, the evening ritual of the baguette was at stake. Joe had wondered if it was his imagination or if the two of them had spent just a fraction longer, a quarter-second only maybe, entangled together on the pavement than the accident strictly warranted.

'Tu n'as pas mal?' the other had said to him. Joe replied that he was not hurt at all, absurdly pleased by the *tu* that had slipped out, unguarded, in place of the more appropriate *vous*.

'You work here?' Joe had enquired.

'My first day,' the other had answered, suddenly sorrowful.

'There's nothing to worry about. *C'était un beau commencement.* My name's Joe. And yours?'

Joe had found himself looking at a young man of about twenty who faced him steadily, a frankness in his eyes that moved him unexpectedly, irrationally, almost to tears. The young man had drawn himself up as if at roll-call in the army. 'Hardrier,' he'd said, adding as if after a comma, 'Antoine.'

'So there it was,' Joe concluded. 'It was instantaneous on both sides. I can't explain how. It just was. His name's Antoine. He's a *mitron*.'

'A Mitterand?' I queried, imagining a relative of the President of the Republic.

'A *mitron*. It's an old word for a baker's boy. The mitrons are still one of the sights of Paris in the early morning, padding round the streets in shorts with their baskets of bread. It's one of the things that make going to work bearable on a winter's morning –though I appreciate that the spectacle might have less of an appeal for you. Antoine works in the boulangerie, in other words.'

For some reason I began to laugh. 'Smitten with a shop boy,' I said. 'It's too funny. I'm sorry to laugh but it is. Sometimes I think you lot are just unreal. In and out of bed one minute, in and out of love the next. Or so you'd have us believe. Why can't you face the truth? You fancy him and that's all. Don't get me wrong now. I'm not going to go all prim and proper on you. There's room in the world for a bit of honest lust. But if only you and your kind would *be* honest and see it for what it is. Don't go confusing things and calling it love.'

'Well, well.' This time Joe did sound nettled. 'Your experience with that French guy does seem to have unhinged you. For someone who knows nothing and would like to know even less about 'us lot' as you call us, you seem to have some pretty definite opinions on the subject. Two days ago you were all ignorance and bliss. You seem very good at shifting your areas of knowledge when it suits you. And, *en plus*, I've never heard you come out with such slurping generalisations on any other subject before. Where the hell's your English talent for equivocation disappeared to? It was still around last Sunday.'

Joe's answer was unsurprising and well-merited, as I realised at once. Why then my strange outburst? I didn't recognize it as coming from myself. It was an odd way for anyone to respond to a friend's announcement that he had fallen in love. 'I'm sorry, Joe,' I said after a moment's reflection.

'Are you jealous?' Joe enquired politely.

Jealous which way round? I wondered. Jealous that Joe was not in love with *me*? Perish the thought! Jealous because I might find the idea of a shop boy attractive, with or without a bread-trolley, myself? Hardly. Jealous of Joe in looks then? Not that either; I considered myself to be better favoured in that respect. What then?

'Perhaps I was a little,' I said slowly. 'I mean jealous that you've found something I have not.'

We walked together up the rue des Archives, brought closer together by the silence that followed my admission than by anything that Joe might have said for answer.

We were going to the Figeac. Joe, having heard the story of Dominique and the 'murder' coming so soon after the episode with Fabrice, had found his curiosity thoroughly aroused and wanted to meet the cast. I stopped as we turned out of the rue des Archives and came in sight of the restaurant. 'How old is he?' he asked.

'Nineteen,' Joe said.

'And you've only met the once?'

'Well no. I buy my bread from him every evening for a start. And I plucked up the courage to ask him to meet me for a *bière de mars* on Saturday. He did. He insisted it must be a bar where neither of us was known. That wasn't so easy in the *quartie*r but we found one in the end. And we talked for a long time.' Joe paused. 'Just that. We talked for a long time.' There was another silence during which we got as far as the restaurant door. 'Well, all right, eventually we went back to my place and went to bed. But it isn't just a little roll in the hay, Peter,' said Joe. 'You'll see.'

We reached the door of the restaurant. I stopped Joe from going straight in. 'I'm glad you're with me,' I said. 'There was a note from Fabrice with my post this morning. Saying the weekend thing's off this time round and could we make it another time. And he said he'll be here in the restaurant this evening. So it'll be nice not to be all alone, if you see what I mean.' I hadn't told Joe anything about that late-night kiss on the cheek of course.

'I can't wait to meet him,' Joe said, with what proportion of sincerity to irony I couldn't tell. Then we pushed open the door and went in and there was everybody. It made a busy, startling contrast to the intimacy of the street.

Taking friends to a favourite restaurant is often a disappointing business. Sometimes it has changed hands the previous day, or it is the chef's night off, or the kitchen is being redecorated and everything smells of paint. I was relieved, then, to find the Figeac exactly as I'd seen it on my other visits, and peopled with more or less the same characters like a stage set. Jean-Jacques leant over the bar in his crow-black coat, nursing a kir, *Libération* spread wide on the wood topped counter. Madame Touret herself presided behind the bar, beaming a professional welcome, while Dominique hovered at a little distance, unsure whether to present himself or to wait for me to approach first. I introduced Joe.

'I'm sorry about your ship,' Dominique said.

'It wasn't really mine,' said Joe.

I explained. 'Joe isn't British, he's American. My ship, if you like, but not his.' The previous day the Herald of Free Enterprise had sunk in Zeebrugge harbour with the loss of 149 lives.

'No, you're right, Joe,' Dominique said, after a

moment's thought. 'There's no such thing as a British ship or a French one, or American or Belgian. Ships are the gossamer strands that join our countries. It's a *connerie* to say anyone owns a ship. They can wear their pennants bravely at the stern – Tricolor, Union Jack or whatever – but all they can do in the end is flutter in the wind.' Dominique shrugged, and grinned apologetically, as if to indicate that there was no arguing with such an obvious fact, then drifted away to join Jean-Jacques.

Joe looked at me in puzzlement. 'What was all that meant to mean?'

'It means he's his usual self again. Come on, let's eat.'

Fabrice and Régine joined us at the table, Fabrice showing not a flicker of awkwardness. To my surprise I felt none either. The couple examined the food on my plate and on Joe's, openly and unselfconsciously asking questions about it. What kind of steak was that? How salty were the beans today? Last Thursday René had used too heavy a hand, Régine explained. Was the salad really fresh? Only then did they give their orders to Madame Touret.

'You got my note, I hope,' said Fabrice, blue eyes shining. Had he really forgotten last weekend's awkwardness and that second, gentler kiss he'd given me, or had an ingrained habit of deception turned him into a consummate actor? 'This weekend's impossible for my parents. Anyway, I was being stupid about the dates. Shooting's already at an end as far as game's concerned. But we can take pot shots at rabbits any time.

So, can we make it in a week or two?' He smiled towards Joe. 'You too if you like. Fancy a bit of rabbit shooting?'

'Tell you what,' Joe answered. 'If crack-shot here' he jerked a thumb towards me 'doesn't make a total fool of himself the first time, I'll come next time round.'

'You're on,' said Fabrice.

Régine turned to me. 'Fabrice was telling me you came to lunch on Sunday,' she said. 'It's nice that he has such good friends in Paris. He gets lonely when I go away.' At this point I did find myself beginning to blush. I focused my attention firmly on my plate so no-one should see. It was a minute or two before I dared to catch Joe's eye.

Fabrice felt compelled to change the subject. 'It was terrible news about your ship,' he said.

During the meal a new face arrived at the bar counter: male, Hispanic, good-looking in a sharp-featured sort of way. 'Who is he?' asked Françoise who by now had joined us. 'Does anybody know?' No-one did, at least no-one at our table, but Dominique was talking to him so he evidently knew him or soon would do. We asked him, when the newcomer had gone.

'He's a cousin of your concierge, Peter,' Dominique explained. 'Arrived yesterday from Portugal. Did you see the gold around his neck and wrists? He says he made a lot of money selling time-shares. Well, believe that if you like. If you ask me he's looking for a job as a concierge... Sorry, we're supposed to say *gardien* now. Anyway I told him to go and talk to the two *ouistitis*... Not both at the same time of course.'

I explained about the belligerent marmosets, Carlos and Nico, on the way back to my flat. I had invited Joe up for a coffee and digestif before he headed back home.

I gave Joe a quick tour of my studio and he turned his attention to the view from the window over the neighbouring roof tops. I put on my Beethoven tape. Then, just as I had done a few nights earlier, Joe noticed the single lighted dormer window outlined against the inky sky. 'That makes a pretty picture,' he said. 'The colours, the contrast of the light and the night, could be Van Gogh.'

'Take sugar?' I asked him. He said, 'Yes please. Who lives there, do you know?'

'In the attic window? I haven't the faintest idea.'

'I just wonder,' Joe said as I poured the coffee, 'if that might not be the question that brought you here to France.'

NINE

Paris. Spring. 1987

Spring was coming and the trees that bordered the overhead Métro lines had turned a lovely translucent green overnight. That this effect of sudden spring was produced not by leaves but by catkins – as could be seen on closer inspection – did not detract from the marvel of it. On the contrary, as Joe explained to me, it exemplified a particularly Parisian trait: turning nature's little deceptions to advantage. If you could not actually have trees in full leaf at forty-nine degrees north in mid-March, you could at least cheer the heart with trees that looked it.

Forsythia followed, in sudden explosions of yellow along the boulevards, and just in the last few days the plane trees appeared to have been hung with emeralds. Day by day the sun was exploring a little further down the walls of the houses. In the clefts of streets that Haussman seemed to have cut with a cheese wire through the city, so deep and regular were they, it advanced with military precision in straight lines. Here in the Marais by contrast, where the old houses leaned backwards at different degrees from the vertical, the sun encroached in sudden spurts, building up gradually a pattern of wedges and spears of light and shade. As the sun fingered its way down in places to street level, so café tables were beginning to sprout from the pavement where it touched. The street life of the spring and summer could tentatively begin.

*

Joe and I were sitting outside the Little Horseshoe, waiting for Fabrice and Régine to join us for a drink before going on to eat at the Figeac. If you sat at any café table long enough Dominique would join you eventually, bringing with him a breath of something from a less predictable world and seating himself without asking in one of the chairs you were saving for Régine and Fabrice. He arrived now.

By way of conversation, and because he had just noticed one shambling up the street, Joe asked Dominique how he dealt with *clochards*. I'm afraid I had to ask what a *clochard* was.

'Not what they were,' Dominique answered. 'The *Cloche* was once an honourable vocation, the clochard a real gentleman of the road. Some were artists, some gipsies, some recluses like mobile monks. They had their codes, their signs, their rules. But in Paris now a clochard is just a beggar, wine-soaked, sleeping in a doorway.'

'I'm with you,' I said. 'There's one sleeps over a warm-air vent outside Madame Almuslih's shop.'

'That's my one,' said Dominique.

'What do you mean, your one?' Joe and I both asked.

Dominique laughed. 'This is the answer to your

question, … er …'

'Joe,' I reminded him.

'Joe. You ought to be generous sometimes and give them what you can. That's not morality, it's common sense. French proverb: 'You never know when you're going to have need of someone smaller than yourself.' But that's where the problem starts. There are so many. What do you do? Try to give something to each one you meet? Impossible. One in every ten? Too calculating. I arrived at an answer. I chose just one. I slip him a coin or two every other day. And because I know him I have the advantage of knowing what he spends it on.'

'Which is...?' I asked.

'Bottles of La Villageoise red from Madame Almuslih's shop. The profit on the sale helps to feed her family. So everybody benefits. He's happy when he's drunk so let him stay drunk. Madame Almuslih's happy when she makes a profit so let her do that. Think of it the other way round and you'll see it would never do at all: Madame Almuslih drunk and the clochard putting money in the bank. No, no. It's better the way it is.'

Fabrice and Régine turned up just then and Dominique reached round, without standing up, for an extra chair. By the time that hands had been shaken (Fabrice's), cheeks kissed (Régine's), and everyone was settled it had dawned on me – at last – that not only was Joe a little bit interested in Fabrice, but that Fabrice returned the compliment. Perhaps it was something in the air of the Marais.

But conversation wasn't allowed to develop very far before we became aware of a scene developing at the bar behind us and we were all very soon screwed round in our seats to watch what was going on. It was the two marmosets.

Nico had been inside the Horseshoe for some time, was slightly the worse for wear, and was beginning to sing the praises of his native Portugal quite loudly to anyone who cared to listen. Had he seen that his Spanish sparring partner was at the other end of the bar he might not have started, but it was rather dark in there and he never did see very well after the seventh glass and it was too late to stop now anyway, because he had already got his captive audience. Carlos was literally captive because of the confined space; he could not discreetly leave the bar without pushing past Nico, which would have defeated the object of the manoeuvre. So he stayed where he was, chin just visible above the counter, and kept silent while the glories of Portugal were lauded together with the exploits of her famous sons. Until, that is, it came to Columbus.

'I think I should point out,' said Carlos in a voice as soft as a feather duster, 'that Christopher Columbus was Italian.'

Nico ignited. 'How typically Spanish! You claim everyone's national heroes as your own because you have none yourselves. Even General Franco was a Moroccan.'

Carlos kept his cool. 'Did I say Columbus was a Spaniard?' He appealed to the room at large. 'Did I?' It was generally agreed that he had not.

Nico could not see the difference for the moment between Italy and Spain. Carlos had contradicted him and that was enough. *'Ta gueule,'* Carlos told him but it was Carlos who in fact stayed silent while Nico continued to blaze like a small box of sparklers. Finally Carlos took two steps towards him and in a voice still feather-soft said, *'Va te faire enculer.'*

There was a moment's general silence. Then Nico said, 'Luckily for you I know your French isn't good enough for you to know what that expression means. Otherwise I'd kill you.'

But Carlos did understand what the expression meant. He proved this by explaining it in elaborate anatomical detail and reinforced it with a mime using his two hands.

Nico stepped back a pace to give himself room to aim and flung his glass and its contents at the other's chest. The glass bounced off onto the floor and shattered. Carlos took the beer itself full in the face. The bystanders were given further evidence of his command of French. A second more and the two marmosets had thrown their jackets on the floor and were squared up to each other, fists ready, dancing from foot to foot.

Then it was Dominique who stood up, in an unexpected assumption of the role of man of action, slipped between them and separated them by the length of his extended arms, one hand against each tiny chest, no higher than his own waist. Someone else grabbed Nico from behind and bundled him out of the door like a scrapping cat. 'I'm going to get a knife,' he said as he unceremoniously left.

Carlos rolled his eyes and shrugged, his hands spread wide. He waited till he had the undivided attention of all present before delivering his final word. 'It's very fortunate for all concerned,' he said, 'that Columbus wasn't Spanish.'

We moved off after that towards the Figeac, the four of us who had arranged to meet, plus Dominique, for whom plans and arrangements didn't seem to exist. As we walked, Fabrice renewed his invitation to me to spend a weekend in Alsace with him and Régine in two weeks' time. Reassured by the thought that Régine would be there, I accepted without anxiety and said I was looking forward to it.

*

On the thirtieth of March Margueritte d'Alabouvettes telephoned from Tokyo to say that she would be passing through Paris in two days time and if I could arrange to have the rent ready in cash she would call by for it. I was invited to an audience with her during the afternoon in one of her two first-floor flats. One of her daughters was with her. Till now we had not progressed beyond *bonjour*. *'Je vous présente ma fille,'* said Margueritte, 'Madame Guyot.'

She opened a bottle of champagne. 'To welcome you to Paris a month late,' as she put it. We sat on sofas and sipped. We smoked menthol cigarettes.

I wondered for a second if I could tell her the story of the two *ouistitis* and Christopher Columbus but quickly decided against. Nor did I mention that Margueritte's concierge, Luisa, had had her cousin staying with her now for three weeks – the cousin who claimed he made a fortune selling time-shares – and that she was at her wits' end to know how to get rid of him. 'He's no good,' she had said. 'Always in trouble with the police at home and now he has to come to France to stir things up. If only someone would take him off my hands.'

I'd later been presented with a moral dilemma when I'd walked into the Figeac to find him, the gold-braceleted Portuguese, dining à deux with Françoise, who was dressed to the teeth and still presumably dreaming of a man who would take her to the sun. Should I do Françoise a favour and tell her what Luisa said, or do Luisa a favour by letting things take their course? In the end I said nothing. If anything is more cordially loathed than an unwelcome truth it is the person who delivers it.

But such stories were not what tenants like me told *propriétaires* like Margueritte over champagne. Instead I handed over the rent money. I'd collected it that morning from the bank in crisp hundred-franc notes all fastened together with a shiny new pin like a kebab. 'You wouldn't happen to have it in notes of five hundred?' said Margueritte d'Alabouvettes.

TEN

An hour after that I was on the train to Saverne with Régine and Fabrice. I told them how my landlady had flown halfway around the world for the rent. Fabrice said that was typical. 'And who is Monsieur Guyot, in the end?' I asked. 'I've now got as far as meeting his wife.'

'His ex-wife,' Fabrice corrected. 'They're separated and she won't give him a divorce. He'd like to screw the d'Alabouvettes for every sou he can. Not that he needs it. He's a big wheel in one of the ministries... Which one is it?' he asked Régine.

'Town Planning and Housing,' she replied. 'But he's moving shortly. He's going to be some sort of functionary at the Elysée Palace, working for *Ton-ton* himself.

'Who's Ton-ton?' I asked.

'President Mitterand,' said Fabrice. He added in English: 'It's his nick-name. Ton-ton means, like, uncle.' Then he gave me one of those brilliant smiles of his that lit up his whole face.

We were met at Saverne station by Fabrice's father, in immaculate suit and tie, at the wheel of a newish-looking Mercedes. I half expected to hear the line about having to bring the Merc because all the other cars were in use. It didn't come. Fabrice's father rose a notch in my estimation.

It took only a few minutes to reach the family home. At the edge of a village, as Fabrice had described it, it nevertheless seemed separate from the other houses, being built not in the local vernacular, half-timbered, style but was an example of restrained eighteenth-century elegance in light-coloured stone with white-painted shutters. Had it been shorn of those and transplanted across the Channel, you would have said Georgian without a second thought. It fronted almost directly onto the road. All the land, said Fabrice – and I had to trust him on that because it was getting dark – lay at the back.

There was a homely family supper of choucroute, which I had once made the mistake of describing to a French person as a version of sauerkraute, only to be told that it was absolutely the other way round and the French did it ten times better anyway. I didn't repeat that error this evening.

What a touching honour it is to be taken to meet a new friend's family. All those intimate parts of a person's life, screened out when you meet them at work or in their own adult homes, are exposed in all their vulnerability to the outsider's potentially cold stare. I hadn't guessed that Fabrice had a little sister still in her teens whom Fabrice obviously adored. Nor that his mother, before marriage, had been a professional musician.

Still less had I imagined that after dinner and a few

glasses of very fine wine, the family would sit down and make music together in nineteenth-century bourgeois tradition. That the teenage sister would play Mozart on the piano. That Régine would, after a suitable show of mock reluctance, sing a selection of numbers from Offenbach operettas in a very passable mezzo voice, accompanied by Fabrice's mother – her own mother-in-law to be? – and that after that Fabrice would be cajoled into singing something himself.

His reluctance seemed to be quite genuine. 'I really don't do this awfully well. And it's doubly unfair to make me follow Régine.' But he got out of his seat like a good lamb going to the slaughter, conferred with his mother for a moment and announced, 'Schubert. *Gute Nacht.*'

Fabrice actually did it rather nicely. He had a naturally pleasing tenor voice and a comfortable musicality even if his technique let him down occasionally on difficult corners. I'd never guessed that this was part of him. We'd never thought to discuss music in the short time we'd known each other. Fabrice sang the song in German, but I knew the story by heart anyway. 'Love loves to wander,' the words reminded more than once. 'From one love to another. God has made it so.' But when Fabrice came to the part where the lover tiptoes from his mistress's bedroom to wander the snowy landscape in search of a new life, and delivered the lines impartially around the room, I found myself hoping that the choice of song was a coincidence and that there was not a hidden message in it from Fabrice to me.

The Paris Novel

I was forced to admit, when they asked me, that I neither sang, nor played an instrument, nor painted. All I could do was write. 'But,' and perhaps it was the wine that prompted this odd announcement, 'I do have very beautiful dreams sometimes.' This went down far better than I thought it might, or deserved to, and Fabrice's mother said, 'Perhaps that's better than all the rest put together,' and smiled in a way that suggested she really meant it.

At bedtime I discovered that Fabrice and Régine went to separate rooms. The parents must know that they lived as a couple in Paris, but presumably traditional proprieties were still observed in the family home. Or maybe it was simply that Fabrice's bedroom was still the one he had had as a child, with a narrow bed in it and teddy bears and model racing cars still stuffed into odd corners of cupboards and drawers. The thought of that made me smile as I undressed for bed in the small but comfortable room they'd given me. There was no lock on the door, I noticed, and was then immediately cross with myself for thinking to look for one.

Next morning we were soon out of doors in brilliant sunshine, me learning to load a shotgun and squinting along its barrel for the first time in my life. Fabrice had lent me a pair of boots and an old Barbour jacket from England so that I looked the part perfectly. The only trouble was that everything of Fabrice's that I had about me was a fairly noticeable two sizes too large.

Rabbit shooting was not Régine's thing, so there were just Fabrice and me and, to my slight surprise, the kid sister, Stéphanie, out in the undulating meadows that lay below the forest-crested hills. Rabbits there were aplenty, though, and their numbers remained unchanged even after I fired my first two experimental shots. After that Fabrice bagged three and Stéphanie, who was considered too young to shoot, acted as a two-legged gun dog and ran and picked them up. But then I got my eye in and, no longer surprised by the kick in the chest that went with recoil, found my next shot rewarded with the sight of a pair of sprinting ears disappearing below the tops of the grass stems, then heard Fabrice's voice sing out, '*Sacré bleu, monsieur.* You've got a hare!'

I tried not to feel too pleased with myself. I suggested that the hare should stay with Fabrice's family as a thank-you present for having me for the weekend. Fabrice wouldn't hear of it. They had no end of hares and rabbits here, whereas in Paris…

'Oh sure,' I said. 'You can just see me cooking a hare for myself in Margueritte's attic, can't you, fur coat and all.' Fabrice assured me he'd take care of all that. We'd have a party for which Fabrice would do the cooking. As for the fur coat and ears, that part would all be sorted out before we even left for the capital.

There was a lunch party for a number of hunting, shooting and fishing neighbours. At which I would have expected to find myself very much out of place but for the fact of having wielded a gun and shot my own hare for the first time just an hour earlier. So I waded into the unfamiliar milieu with a bit of self-confidence and found that I enjoyed another un-suspected advantage: that of being the only person there who hadn't been wining and dining with all the others for a lifetime and listening to one another's old stories until they knew them by heart.

'We've got a mobile phone,' said one white-haired landowner lady to a little group of similar others. A mobile was still a novelty then. 'And Isolde rang the other day. You know how she talks. Well, I was in the bath. After a while the water started getting cold. I started moving to try to splash it round a bit. 'You sound as if you're in the sea,' Isolde said. 'It's not the sea,' I told her. 'I'm in the bath.' *Je vous assure*, no conversation with Isolde has ended more promptly. Try it sometime.'

There were younger people too. One couple, about Fabrice and Régine's age, who had a farm a dozen kilometres away, invited them and me to join them for an aperitif later, in the early evening. There would be a number of other people there: people Fabrice had been to school with. A day before, I'd have said this was the last thing that I and my creaky French would want to cope with during a relaxing weekend, but I was buoyed with satisfaction at the way things had gone up to now, and especially having caught my first hare, and found myself looking forward to it. Getting to know Fabrice was turning out more enjoyable than I had expected at first, and I decided that having met his family it might be interesting to talk to people from his past as well.

The afternoon was a short one. It consisted of brief but welcome siestas, everybody in their own rooms, and then a game of table football in the basement games room. Régine was particularly good at this. But then, at the last minute, when it was time to set out for the pre-prandial drinks party, she pleaded tiredness and would we boys mind dreadfully if she didn't come with us? I did mind just a little, because I had only accepted the invitation on the understanding that I would not be left alone with Fabrice for any length of time. But I couldn't find any excuse to cry off and anyway, it did seem pretty pathetic to be scared of someone who might, just might, make a pass at me. We were only going to drive a few miles together, and Fabrice was hardly going to rape me, after all.

We took the Mercedes. 'We'll go the quick way,' Fabrice said. 'It's a forest back road over the hills. Saves ten minutes over the main road along the valley.' Fabrice clearly wanted to show off his driving skill in the powerful car and, once we'd left the sedate Route Nationale behind, he whizzed us at incautious speed round the hillside-hugging bends with a great show of nonchalance. It was the sort of ride that's more fun for the driver than for any passengers. I wondered whether that was why Régine had decided not to come with us. In the middle of a particularly densely forested stretch Fabrice pointed to a pair of iron gates that interrupted a long red-brick wall. Beyond them a track-way led away through an impenetrable secrecy of conifers. 'You'll be interested to know who lives there,' Fabrice said. 'It's the cousin of Margueritte that my family knows: Pierre-Valéry d'Alabouvettes. Used to be in the government under Giscard. Of course he's retired now. We can't see the house from the road but it's one hell of a château up there in the woods.' An idea struck him. 'We could go over there tomorrow. He actually likes me quite a lot and he's very generous with the booze cabinet. I'll catch him up by phone when we get back tonight.'

'You say him,' I said. 'Does he live up here all alone?'

'He has his secretary living with him, if you understand me.'

'That seems a bit transparent,' I said, 'and yet old-fashioned at the same time. The worst of both worlds. What does she think about that?'

'It isn't a she,' said Fabrice, 'it's a he.'

Five minutes later we had come down from the hills and arrived at a farmhouse, handsome and half-timbered, that would have made a setting for a Grimms' tale. Inside was a crowd of thirty-something people, among whom the blond hair and blue eyes that drew attention to Fabrice in Paris were the rule rather than the exception, and who were circulating in a haze of cigarette smoke – for the garden weather part of the spring day was past – and an ambient scurry of dogs to trip unwary feet.

Although everyone who spoke to me addressed me in French I was aware that a lot of neighbouring conversations took place in the local dialect or *patois* as they called it. I recognized it as a form of German but was too polite to say so. We were served wine, local Sylvaner and Gewurztraminer, which Fabrice and I drank in imprudent quantities, while smoking other people's cigarettes. At least there were titbits to mop the booze up: mainly crisp hot sausages cut into bite-sized portions.

'So Fabrice has found a real Englishman in Paris,' one young woman said to me. 'That'll have pleased him. All his life he's tried to be more British than the Brits. Barbour jackets and Earl Grey tea. Of course you wouldn't have noticed.'

It was true. I hadn't. I started down another track. 'He and Régine. Are they heading for marriage, do you think? It's what, two years they've been together?' I knew I was being nosey, but I felt that my own experience of Fabrice entitled me to a certain curiosity on the subject.

'Probably yes,' said the other. She was attractive in a comfortable, round-faced way and reminded me a little of my last girlfriend but one. 'He never had girlfriends when he was younger, as far as we knew, at any rate. He was a bit of a loner. But late starters often make up for lost time quite energetically. And the two of them seem pretty serious. Where is she by the way?' I explained about her feeling too tired to come. 'The prospect of his driving, more probably,' the young woman said.

Which reminded me that Fabrice would also have to drive us back, after a hefty intake of good Alsatian wine. Well, whatever happened, I told myself, we were in it together. I looked out of the window. I couldn't believe how dark it had become. I was losing track of time. This early aperitif was turning into a full evening. I looked at my watch. No, it was not all that late: only eight o'clock.

Then why was it so dark? I remembered that I was now in the eastern extremity of France where sunrise and sunset both happened that much earlier than in Paris. Perhaps that accounted for it. But Fabrice arrived and refilled my glass just then, and a bright young female student from Strasbourg came up to talk to us both and I forgot my puzzlement.

At last Fabrice noticed the time himself and suggested it was time to leave. Other people began to make a move at the same moment and, as they tumbled out of the opening front door, began to exclaim together in a murmur of *mon dieux* and oohs and aahs. A steady fall of snow was in progress and the ground and bushes were already covered in white. 'But it's April,' I said, startled, 'and this morning was so brilliant.'

'It can happen,' said Fabrice. 'High up here it can happen even in May. But it needn't worry us. We'll take the quick way, the road we came along. We'll be back before it gets to any depth.'

Anthony McDonald

ELEVEN

The depth of snow in the sheltered valley from which we were setting off was very different from the depths we encountered on the high road through the forest that took us back towards Saverne. Snow lay a little more thickly on each ridge of higher ground that we crossed, and by the time we were only halfway back we were ploughing through four inches or more of nearly virgin whiteness. The view ahead was whiteness too, a tunnel of fast-flying flakes that seemed to attack the windscreen only to veer off left, right and upward at the last split second. And the wipers, on double speed, heaved protestingly at fans of settling crystals that grew heavier and more opaque with every stroke. Fabrice kept his foot down and we ploughed grimly on.

Night had really fallen and the headlights picked out just one solitary set of tyre-prints leading the way ahead of us. But even those, our only contact with other traffic on the lonely road, were growing fainter by the second. I realised for the first time that no traffic was coming the other way and I turned round in my seat to confirm my near certainty that no headlights were following us either. 'We're a bit in the middle of nowhere, aren't we?' I said, trying to make my tone conversational.

'Not really.' Fabrice was trying to do the same. 'Another few kilometres and you'll see the lights of Saverne shining up from the valley as we swing round the bends. Then it's downhill all the way home.' But downhill in these conditions seemed an even less comforting prospect than up.

A thwacking sound and the Merc shivered slightly. We'd crashed through a windswept dune of snow that had settled through a gap in the trees. Cold sparks of crystal danced in the headlights for a moment, swirling like galaxies of stars. The next drift loomed up twenty seconds later. The car porpoised through it with a thump. Then the drifts came regularly, like waves, the car transformed into a power boat, sending the semi-solid breakers up in showers of surf as it charged them one by one. 'It's like we're surfing our way home,' said Fabrice, his voice charged with an excitement that had not quite yet been crowded out by fear.

'My God. Look there!' I saw the big one first. The drift was sinuously in motion, solidifying before our eyes out of its own particular micro-blizzard. Its crest was a changing skyline that dissolved into an upward flowing fog of ice. It reared higher than the car as we approached. In a futile gesture of defiance Fabrice slammed his foot down to the floor. We struck. The Merc buffered to a stop. Wheels spun in a high-pitched whine and whir of protest. Fabrice tried reverse. Surprisingly the car inched back a metre or so. Then slewed sideways into deeper snow and stuck. He took it out of gear.

We got out of the car. The drift seemed to have stopped moving; it lay inert as if in shock from our assault on it. Rising little higher than the top of the bonnet it looked remarkably un-threatening: a different animal from the sinister rearing monster that had confronted us through the windscreen a moment ago. But it stretched a limo's length along the road in front of us. There was no shovel in the car, Fabrice confirmed. 'But you've got your mobile phone,' I said. Fabrice was about the only one of my friends who had one.

'Yes, of course,' Fabrice answered. Then, deadpan, 'I left it at my parents'.'

'Oh, right,' I said, nodding calmly, and wondering what on earth we were going to do next. Logically there were only two choices and neither appealed.

'They won't find us till the morning if we stay in the car,' Fabrice said. 'It might be buried by then.'

I stated the obvious. 'And if we keep the engine going for heat we'll die from the monoxide.'

'And if we don't we'll freeze to death.' There was a silence as we stared at each other across the bonnet of the car.

Then Fabrice said, *'T'as pas un clops?'* Got a fag?

'I don't smoke, except for other people's.' I laughed. 'Same as you.' And Fabrice laughed too.

'Look,' Fabrice said, 'we're very near the house I showed you, the château where Pierre-Valéry lives. We can make it easily on foot.'

I looked along the road ahead. But for the impenetrable blackness of trees on either side I couldn't have seen where its path lay at all. In the car's headlights the snow still fell weightily, in flakes now grown too big for dancing. Beyond the headlights' reach the dark was absolute. 'Do we have a torch?'

There was one in the car, mercifully. Only large pocket size but infinitely better than nothing. Almost better, there was a coat – though only one. Neither of us had more on than a shirt and jacket, jeans and casual shoes. Fabrice lifted the coat out of the boot. It was an ancient Afghan affair, half a generation old, with holes in it, and although it had moulted much of its own original hair this had been replaced in some measure by an encrustation of dog hairs that had accumulated over the course of a long and useful afterlife as a car blanket for family canines. Fabrice held it up apologetically. 'Best we can do, I'm afraid. We can't both fit into it though.'

'We could wear it in turns,' I said. 'Five minutes each.'

Reluctantly we switched off the car's lights and the ignition. The finality of the blackness and the silence that followed this appalled us and left us for a little while unable to move or speak. Then Fabrice threw me the coat – 'You first,' – shone the torch ahead of us, and we moved off.

Along the right-hand side of the road the drift was shallower. We waded through it up to our knees. I attempted a black joke. 'Lucky we're not in Wellingtons. Snow would have come in over the top.' Not only no boots. No pullovers, no scarves, no gloves.

The going was easier beyond the drift: the snow lay only a few inches deep. But then there came the next drift and the next. I was conscious of the presence of the car behind us, our only connection to a world beyond this white one, but silent now and dark and dead, receding into uselessness like an abandoned talisman with every step we took. I was tempted to take the torch from Fabrice and shine it behind us to see how far we'd come since leaving the Mercedes. Then I remembered Lot's wife and changed my mind.

In only a few minutes we were both shivering and wet. With a jolt I remembered the coat we were supposed to be sharing. I tore it off my back with guilty haste. 'Fabrice, take it.' If I was soaked and freezing then Fabrice must be halfway to hypothermia.

'Come on,' said Fabrice in English. 'It's my fucking fault we're here.'

'I knew there was a road along the valley too,' I said. 'I could have said, take that one.' I threw the coat round Fabrice's shoulders and started manically to stuff his arms into the sleeves as if he were an elderly invalid, until Fabrice accepted the point and finished the task for himself.

'How far did you say?' I asked. In the course of giving up the coat I had somehow acquired command of the torch and it shone still on an unchanging vista of snowdrifts framed by fir trees on either side. I knew quite well that Fabrice hadn't said how far he thought it was and that, in this whited-out forest landscape where we had come to a stop, he couldn't possibly know.

'Not far now,' was his upbeat reply.

He really is more British than the Brits, I thought. 'Perhaps we'll find a lamp post among the fir trees,' I said.

'Why a lamp post?' Fabrice was puzzled.

'It's something in an English children's book.'

'Oh, I know. We have it in French too. About a magic lion. And witches?' Perhaps it was the poignancy of the chance words, children and magic, for Fabrice suddenly reached out his hand for mine and I took it firmly, without protest. 'Conserve a little bit of heat at least, like that,' Fabrice said, and without further discussion we plodded onward hand in hand.

Fabrice didn't bother to look at his watch. He relinquished the coat when he heard my teeth chattering just below his left ear. Then, after what seemed about five more minutes, I handed it back. And so we went on.

It was Fabrice who stopped first. He was panting. 'Just need to get my breath back for a moment.'

'We can't,' I said. 'We'll freeze.'

'Well, you go on. I'll catch you up. I only need a second.'

'Don't be silly,' I said. We were still attached at the hands, and I pulled at Fabrice like a child trying to drag a parent to the sweet-counter until he started moving again.

Much later we consulted my watch by the light of the torch. We had been going for over an hour. The snow was no longer melting on the tops of our heads but clinging there, giving us a white cap each. It plastered our shoulders too and the fronts of our jackets. Only our reversed lapels had kept the worst of it from our shirts and chests. Our progress could no longer be described as walking. We were stumbling along, often using hands to crawl across the deeper drifts. It was no longer a case of holding hands but of using them constantly to pull each other up when we had fallen. We were both falling over now constantly, like farm animals about which the farmer would say the only thing to be done was put them down. Fabrice's numb fingers had let the torch go twice and we'd had to scrabble for it among the tracks our legs and bodies made, finding it thanks to the light it shed so prettily among the miniature caves and canyons we had formed.

Then suddenly I saw it. 'Look there!' The torch, which I was holding now, showed brickwork alongside the road. Brickwork with no ends in sight. 'A wall.' How long we had been following it we had no idea. I waded towards it, touched it, rested my back against it, then found myself sinking down, despite myself, dizzy with exhaustion and the cold.

I came to with Fabrice's voice a breathless shout in my ears. 'Don't do that. Don't stop. You told me that yourself a while back.' Fabrice's arms were hauling me up out of the snow, out of the sleep into which I had been falling, so nicely and so comfortably falling, like a winter dormouse, like a hedgehog, like a smallish bear. '*Viens, viens*, we're nearly there. This is the wall of the estate. Just follow it along and we'll be at the gate. We're there.' He managed something like a laugh. 'Peter, don't die on me now.'

We used the wall for support, creeping along it in snow whose shallowest deposits were now knee-deep. How big could an estate possibly be? How long its boundary wall? Nothing existed for me now except that gate and the unseen great house beyond it. Everything else fell away: weekend in Alsace, Régine, job and life in Paris, home in England and all my past. Nothing mattered any more or had meaning. Fabrice apart, the only thing that existed – I saw it clearly in my mind, though I had only glimpsed it as we rushed by unheeding during that afternoon so long ago, and not attached any importance to it – was that gate. I knew it now. As if my mind had photographed it and was just delivering the prints, I saw it before me. Brick by brick I knew its two supporting pillars and could number their stone quoins. I saw the iron-railed portals with their spikes on top. There were lamps atop the pillars...

Fabrice apart... Fabrice too I could have described in as much detail, without bothering to turn my head. Every hair of his moustache, every laughter-line on his face, every breath of his that exchanged its heat with the frozen air, all was imprinted on my consciousness and fastened there like the icicles that gripped my beard and hair.

The gate came into torch range. It came as powerfully as an apparition, like something supernatural looming through the snow. But the lamps on top of the two pillars were unlit except by the wavering beam of our torch, and the gates themselves, when we pushed at them, were locked.

'We go over the top,' said Fabrice. His voice was hoarse and breathless, thin as a thread. We didn't stop to debate this or even get our breath. We were both fired up with a terrifying sense that delay was just a stepping stone away from death. Fabrice climbed first while I shone the torch. It wouldn't have been difficult ordinarily, except for the spikes, but in his exhausted state he had to struggle to the top. He got one leg over the top of the spikes and was balancing gingerly above them prior to shifting his weight and flipping his other leg across when he let out an animal howl of pain. My blood ran cold. The spikes. I flinched and dropped the torch.

'What?' I called in panic, groping at my feet for the dropped light.

'Cramp. Got cramp.'

'Thank God for that,' I said. 'Thought you'd impaled yourself.' I rescued the torch and shone it up to where Fabrice remained, as immobile and awkward as if he really had skewered himself on the railings. 'I'm coming up.' I started to climb, with the strap of the torch between my teeth. 'Which leg?'

'Your side.'

I found Fabrice's calf and massaged it, first through his jeans and then by putting my hand up under the fabric and rubbing the muscle itself. How reassuringly solid it seemed – the cramp itself was partly responsible for this – and warm. My attentions were more comfort gesture than cure, but in comforting Fabrice I found that I was comforted myself and was startled and almost aggrieved when Fabrice said, 'Thank you, it's OK now,' and vaulted over and down the other side. A second later I had joined him.

It was difficult to guess the direction in which the driveway ran, and there was no sign of a light. 'Do they have dogs?' I asked.

'There used to be a panther.'

'You're joking,' I said, horrified. 'What, loose in the grounds?'

'It was in a cage. It's OK though. It was years ago. They sold it to a zoo.'

The snow was less deep in here. In a businesslike way we found each other's hands again and held them after a fashion as we walked, but our fingers were just hardened ridges of ice and wouldn't clasp.

'Supposing they're away?'

'Don't even think it,' said Fabrice.

Anthony McDonald

And then there was a light...

TWELVE

It seemed almost unreal to be ringing a doorbell. To hear a crackled query from the electric box beside it. To hear Fabrice reciting his full name, hoarsely and urgently, twice. Even more unreal when the door opened and we stumbled, nearly fell, into a hallway so yellow-bright with electricity that it hurt the eyes, so warm that, like a fire, it stung the cheeks. A courteous middle-aged man had let us in. An older one with a long and claret-coloured face and an aristocratic mane of silver hair appeared in a doorway, his mouth opening with astonishment as he saw the state of the travellers who had found their way to his door. *'Mon dieu,'* he said, advancing towards Fabrice. He felt his soaking jacket shoulders and flicked snow from his head onto the floor. He turned to the other man. 'Hervé, get two dressing-gowns immediately.' Then to Fabrice and me. 'Come through at once. Get those clothes off, get by the fire, then some whisky down you. Everything else can wait. Excuse me.' He reached out a hand and flicked the snow off my head too. It joined Fabrice's contribution in a puddle on the tiles.

'I need to phone...' began Fabrice. He was swaying on his feet. I caught him.

'We'll do all that,' said the older man and guided us both through the open door to where a log fire blazed between brass-headed fire-dogs. Hervé reappeared with two towelling bathrobes and laid them side by side on the arm of a sofa. 'Get into these quickly,' he said. 'We won't watch you,' and with an air of having urgent matters to attend to elsewhere, both men left the room.

We looked at each other for a moment, almost apologetically in Fabrice's case, and then started to undress. It was not an easy process. Our clothes clung to us wetly and our fingers were so numb from the cold that when it came to undoing buttons we might as well have been using chopsticks. 'Here, let me.' Fabrice took over when it came to my cuffs and I, really to give myself something to do, returned the compliment. But I made sure to deal with my trousers myself. It was the last stage that presented the most difficulty, though. Trying to remove my socks, I discovered that I couldn't feel my feet and, simultaneously, that taking my socks off was not simply like peeling a banana: the feet themselves played an active part in the process and, unbeknown to me, had been doing so all my life. This evening though, the toes kept snagging themselves in the fabric like the fins of a fish in a landing net. Without a word Fabrice knelt to help me and in a second the process was complete.

'I think I've got frostbite,' I said.

I didn't know the word in French and Fabrice didn't know it in English but he got the general idea. He rubbed my feet gently with one of the bathrobes. 'You'll be all right,' he said. We were both suddenly conscious of being totally naked together for the first time. I couldn't help noticing that Fabrice had a nice physique but I also noticed that his reciprocal gaze was a little more interested than I would have wished. Inevitably my eyes turned to Fabrice's sex. The cold had diminished it to cherubic proportions, nearly lost in a forest of fur. Glancing down I saw that I was in a similar condition. I found myself giving a little uneasy laugh, which Fabrice immediately echoed, and we both relaxed.

'Get this on, for God's sake.' I threw one of the white bathrobes at Fabrice's head and a second later we were decently clad.

As if on cue the two older men returned, Hervé with a tray on which were a bottle of The Macallan single malt and two well filled tumblers which he pressed into our hands, actually helping to arrange our stiffened fingers into a grasp strong enough for the heavy glasses not to fall to the floor.

We fell into, rather than sat upon, one of the deep and encircling sofas, which seemed to enfold us in its silken arms. A small table at each end of it was ready to receive our whisky tumblers when those were not in the process of being raised to our lips, while in front of us the fire glowed in expansive maturity. I was so overcome with the sensation of salvage from the jaws of death that I no longer cared what might happen to me next, or for the rest of my life.

'I've phoned your father to say you're safe,' said the snowy-haired man to Fabrice. 'Then you can phone again in your own time.' He smiled. 'And talk to Régine I guess.' He turned to me. 'Now who do you need to phone?'

'Nobody,' I said 'Nobody knows I'm here.'

'What a chill those words strike in the film-goer,' he replied archly. 'But don't worry. You haven't come to Dracula's castle.'

I looked around me. It was a castle all the same.

Only then did Pierre-Valéry d'Alabouvettes introduce himself, refusing to allow me to stand up while he shook his hand. 'And please, please call me P.V. Fabrice does.'

'I think I know your cousin Margueritte,' I said. 'I'm one of her tenants at the Hôtel des Corbeaux.'

'*Chut*,' said P.V. 'Don't let's hear the word tenant. The unspeakable Charles Guyot will be jumping out of the woodwork at any second with a summons from the *percepteur des taxes*.' He introduced the younger man as, '*Hervé, mon secrétaire*.'

Side by side on the sofa, Fabrice and I could not exchange glances. Instead I felt the warmth of Fabrice's leg pressed for an instant against my own through the two layers of towelling: the leg-language equivalent of a complicit wink.

The whisky was soon gone and refills came quickly. The evening meal had clearly been eaten some time ago, but Hervé was despatched to the kitchen to find what he could in the fridge, do something with it and deliver it to us refugees.

Fabrice left the room to phone Régine and for a few

minutes I found myself alone with P.V. I'd never had a private conversation with a government minister before, not even an ex-one, and wasn't quite sure what to talk about, forgetting momentarily what I already knew from my father and his colleagues on the Northampton Borough Council: namely that politicians are quite capable of setting the conversational agenda themselves.

'What an interesting character our Fabrice is,' the ex-minister began without preamble. 'So charming, so gifted and intelligent ... and so mixed up.' He smiled benignly, like someone in an eighteenth century portrait, and added, 'Don't you find?'

'What do you mean?'

P.V. looked half away from me, perhaps checking there was enough wood on the fire. 'At some point in their lives, everyone has to decide what it is they want, and who they want to be. It's not just a matter of being selfish. It's a question of making things possible for other people.' He looked back at me. 'Rather than making things gradually impossible for them. For Régine, for example. I don't think Fabrice, for all his intelligence, has got round to asking himself one or two questions. Questions that you and I, for example, probably dealt with long ago – though longer ago in my case than in yours. Maybe he finds them a bit hard to ask, or is afraid of the answers.'

I laughed faintly. P.V. continued. 'Maybe you'll turn out to be a benevolent star rising on his horizon. Perhaps you'll be the person who finally sorts him out.'

I said, 'I don't think I'm competent to sort out other people's lives. I actually came to France to sort out my own.'

P.V. smiled. 'You don't have the air of a person with a problematic life, you know. You look too … too young, too charming, too open-eyed. As you say in English, you seem *without sheeps on your shoulder.*'

'All the same,' I said 'I'm getting far more involved in other people's lives than I would really like.' The whisky must have been going to my head.

As if he had just noticed this and was responding appropriately, P.V. got up and poured me another. 'Speaking personally,' he said, 'I'd have thought that dealing with other people's uncertainties was one of the best ways to confront your own.'

Fabrice returned to the room, followed a second or two later by Hervé, who announced that he'd turned on the radiator in the *chambre des pinsons* for the visitors. Fabrice turned to me and explained that each bedroom in the house was named after a different forest bird – ours was the chaffinch room – while Hervé unloaded the tray he had been carrying. There were *omelettes aux cêpes* (tinned cêpes: he apologised) salad, and a baguette cut into chunks. And the wine – it being easier in a castle to find a good bottle than to create gourmet meals at eleven o'clock at night – was a bottle of Volnay Clos des Chênes 1979. I thought: maybe I am dead and there is a heaven after all. And when the bottle was empty, there was another one.

P.V. asked Fabrice for the registration number of his father's car, then went off to the phone to alert the *gendarmerie* to its presence on the forest road. 'Otherwise someone'll smash a snow-plough into it in the morning. That or you'll get a parking ticket.' He was only gone a moment. 'Would you believe it. They weren't the smallest bit interested. Simply said, had you secured the vehicle? As if anyone's going to pinch it, up here, in a snowdrift. In the end I gave them my name, just to make them jump.'

'And did they?' asked Hervé.

'They called me *monsieur* finally. Do you suppose that counts?'

The wine kept coming. I had no objection. I was in anybody's hands now, anyone's but my own. My body had thawed suddenly; my face burned in the fire's heat and my hands and feet had tingled themselves back to some kind of normality. The same processes must have completed themselves for Fabrice; I could feel the warmth of his body next to me, radiating through my *robe de chambre*.

'We're keeping you up,' said Fabrice eventually. 'You've been incredibly good to us.' Mumblingly I echoed his thanks. We were shown up creaking stairs to the *chambre des pinsons*. It was more like a suite than a room, comprising ante-chamber, bathroom and bedroom, all carpeted and sumptuous. Not only was it extremely warm thanks to Hervé's earlier prompt attention to the radiator control, there was also a small token log fire in the hearth, which seemed to express in its exuberant manner of burning a kind of astonishment at its own sudden kindling.

One enormous double bed occupied a large part of the principal chamber. It looked comfortable and welcoming, with a corner of the top sheet turned down. I felt it would have been ungrateful to ask for a separate bed.

'I'll leave you to it,' said Hervé, without innuendo so far as I could tell. 'No hurry in the morning. Sleep it out.'

We were alone. Standing close together, we looked at each other for a moment, but finding it uncomfortable to meet each other's gaze we both turned to look around us instead. Three of the bedroom walls were fitted with mirrors, small ones and large ones in semi-Gothic frames. They were old and not all perfectly aligned, so that as the two of us rotated slowly in opposing arcs, we found ourselves confronted by image after image of ourselves, together and separately, viewed from every conceivable angle, in every imaginable point of rotation away from and towards each other. Two young men, one somewhat bigger than the other, the smaller one bearded, the other merely moustached, both with unkempt blondish hair, both wrapped in nothing but white towelling *robes de chambre*.

The mirrors behind us finally, we faced the reality of each other once more face to face. And now we read clearer, if still cautious, signals in each other's eyes.

The Paris Novel

Tentatively Fabrice put his hands on my shoulders. 'You saved my life out there,' he said. His bathrobe, no longer held together, had fallen open at the front. His cock was visible in the gap. It was thickening up.

'You saved *my* life,' I said, then stepped forward and embraced him, and was conscious of my chest encountering the warmth of Fabrice's as we began to kiss.

This isn't happening, I told myself. I thought about the naked couple I'd spied upon during my first evening in Paris. About my voyeuristic promenade along the quai des Tuileries. I told myself – this is just a one-off. Something that just occasionally happens to people once in life. Extreme circumstances. Mates who've faced ordeals together, celebrating life and solidarity and victory in the only appropriate way. It happened in the army sometimes, I knew. It would never happen again of course. Not to me. But for now, well my cock, like Fabrice's, was hard and upstanding

What would I feel about this in the morning, when Burgundy and whisky and adrenalin and everything had all worn off? I refused to contemplate that now. If this was never to happen to me again – and I was determined that it wouldn't happen again – I was going to experience it to the full now.

It was not only moustache and lips and chest and belly and fur that pressed against me. I could feel my hardness between us and Fabrice's too: together creating something double-barrelled like binoculars, like the shotgun of this morning, today, so long ago. Hard yet giving, so quite unlike the shotgun really, firmly together yet separable too.

We stood without even the pretend modesty of half-worn bathrobes. Those lay behind our heels. We looked at each other for the first time with undisguised approbation and desire. Fabrice's clothes had been a size or two bigger than mine and the same went for all those other things of his that I hadn't seen or touched before tonight: chest and biceps, thighs and cock. But I felt I had nothing myself to be ashamed of. I was as well-proportioned, on my smaller scale, as Fabrice. 'You're beautiful,' Fabrice said suddenly in English. The words gave me a frisson. I knew that he'd said it in English for a purpose. He wanted a nuance more precise than *Tu es beau*.

'Whatever you want,' he said quietly when we had rough-and-tumbled each other onto the bed, and he lay back sensually, spread-eagled and relaxed upon it as if we were about to play a board game to which I was a newcomer and therefore allowed to be the first to cast the dice.

I knew what to do. I'd seen it done. I found the anatomical novelty of the situation less problematic or off-putting than I'd imagined. I wet my cock with spittle and pushed it into the place that Fabrice was offering to me, between the cheeks of his butt. It slipped in with reassuring ease. Fabrice took responsibility for pleasuring himself, almost literally in my face. I might have expected to find that a turn-off but to my surprise it actually increased my excitement. It was more than two months since I'd had sex with anyone except myself. Perhaps because of that it was over all too soon. I came inside Fabrice as quickly as a teenager. Then Fabrice let fly his load, just beneath my face. I slumped forward and lay limp on Fabrice's wet chest. Again I said, 'You saved my life.'

'You idiot,' Fabrice said gently. 'It was me that put your life at risk. And you saved me.' I wasn't quite sure now, though I hardly cared, if we were talking about our adventure in the snow or something else. I found that I was crying. Fabrice began to stroke the back of my head, and I discovered with a finger that my own tears were not the only ones that rolled down Fabrice's cheeks.

Anthony McDonald

THIRTEEN

The morning brought a cloudless blue sky and warm sunshine. It was late when we surfaced and the snow was already thawing rapidly, falling off trees and roofs in lumps as big as duvets.

I was surprised to find in myself no sign yet of the successive waves of self-hatred and guilt that I had expected would set in as soon as day dawned. There would be plenty of time for all that later, I told myself. Those feelings would no doubt steal up on me at a moment of their own choosing, like a delayed hangover – and after last night's intake I fully anticipated one of those too. But perhaps the situation I found myself in played a role in this. To wake up in a castle in Alsace on a diamantine morning of spring snow was very different from finding myself, for example, in an urban bedsit, making awkward conversation over soggy Cornflakes. And then there was the question of Fabrice. I looked at him sideways as we stood together looking out of the window, both wearing those towelling dressing-gowns again because we had nothing else.

The damage was done. I'd gone to bed with a man, had had sex with that man and enjoyed it. None of that new extension to the fabric of my life could be unpicked. But at least the man in question was a handsome, masculine one, intelligent and affectionate. I still thought so as I looked at him this morning. So it could have been worse. Just.

There was a knock at the door. It was Hervé. 'I saw you both at the window...' His face broke into an unplanned grin as soon as he was in the room with us. Perhaps the events of the night were only too legible in our faces, our body language, or even the state of the bed. But then he mastered his facial muscles and handed us the clothes that we'd been wearing when we arrived. They were now dry. There would be breakfast downstairs as soon or as late as we wanted it. Meanwhile the road beyond the gates had been ploughed and the estate manager, who had just finished clearing the driveway, was at the ready with the tractor to take us back to our abandoned car and help us get it moving once more.

As we began to dress, I ran into trouble again with my socks. The two smallest toes would keep snagging; I seemed to have no control over them at all. Fabrice saw this. 'OK, let me.' Still naked, he bent down and manipulated my socks carefully over my recalcitrant feet. That accomplished he stood up, then seized me and kissed me. I found myself submitting to this quite philosophically and even kissed him back. After all, it was absolutely certain that we would never again stand naked together like this. 'It worries me,' said Fabrice, 'how you're going to manage this sock business tomorrow morning when you have to dress yourself.' And then, partly because of the way Fabrice said that, it began to worry me too.

We rode out in borrowed coats and boots and gloves, one on each mudguard of the tractor, and holding tight to the shovel we each carried, and which our shaking progress threatened to dislodge from our grasp and grind under-wheel into the snow. The Merc, when we found it just two miles away, looked like a minor mammoth that had come to a sticky end encased in ice. The snowplough's path had snaked around it leaving it walled up behind the embankment of cleared snow.

After an energetic fifteen minutes the car was cleared from its drift, a tow rope was attached and the tractor dragged the icebound vehicle into the ploughed middle of the road. To everyone's surprise it started up at once – Fabrice had sensibly removed a small souvenir of snowdrift from the exhaust before attempting this – and, following the tractor, Fabrice drove it and me slowly back to the castle in the woods.

Playing the chevalier to the last, Pierre-Valéry offered us an aperitif before we finally set off, but it was nearly one o'clock by now and we said a polite no and took the road again, to rejoin Fabrice's family and Régine for Sunday lunch. After that would come the train ride back to Paris.

Alone with Fabrice in the car – we'd be back at his house in ten minutes or so, barring accidents on the ice – I decided to broach the subject of our adventure together in the *chambre des pinsons*. 'Look,' I said. 'I don't want you to think that what happened last night is usual for me. I was acting a bit out of character. Perhaps you were too.' I waited for Fabrice to confirm my optimistic interpretation of the facts, but he didn't and I was forced to go on. 'I'm not bisexual – which maybe at some level you are.' This time Fabrice grunted non-committally: it might have been possible to interpret this as an assent, though perhaps not in a court of law. 'Last night was a one-off. I was in a state. We both were. It was an emotional response to an exceptional situation. We came close to dying on that road – on this road. You did save my life. You say I saved yours, well, I don't know. But it made a difference – just for last night, just that one night – to the way I felt about … well, everything.' I stopped again. Fabrice was obstinately silent, excused conversation perhaps by the concentration required to drive on the still treacherous white surface of the road among the hills. I continued. 'To be honest, I have to say it probably wouldn't have happened if you'd been anyone else. You're not only a good friend, but you have beautiful eyelashes too, if you see what I mean.' I looked sideways at Fabrice. It was no less than the truth. Still Fabrice kept his own eyes resolutely on the road. I went on. 'You'd better make the most of that compliment, though, because I'm not going to repeat it. And I'm not going to repeat the experiment with you either, in case you're wondering. Not with you or with anybody else. And, if we're going to stay friends, then I don't want to talk about what happened last night ever again, either between ourselves or with anyone else. Do you – can you – understand that?'

'You want to bury it, in other words. Entomb the whole experience in ice.' It was probably the landscape and our experience with the car that prompted Fabrice to so graphic a metaphor.

'Since you put it like that, yes I do. And so should you. If – I'm sorry to be blunt – if you value your relationship with Régine – and I mean for the long term – then you should forget it too.'

'You being the great guru on the subject of successful long-term relationships, I suppose. Sorry to be blunt.' It was the first time I'd heard Fabrice say anything even remotely critical of, or to, anybody. It stung the more for that.

We drove in silence for another minute, negotiating the looping bends that led the forest road down from its heights to rejoin the main road at the bottom, then Fabrice said, 'Your secret is safe. I won't blab about this to anyone – ever, or claim you as any sort of conquest, and, because I want to stay your friend, I'll do what you ask and never mention it again between us, unless you do first – which, by the way, is not as improbable as you may think right now. But I won't forget it, or bury it away. I'll remember it always as one of the great adventures of my life. I nearly died in the company of a beautiful, sexy young man who's more or less straight, like me, and he saved my life, and we spent the night in a castle and we made love. Nothing too complicated or alarming about that, I'd have thought. Only beautiful. And who did what to whom is just a detail. No, I'll never forget it. I'll remember it in any case tomorrow morning when I put my socks on. And I promise you, so will you.' He couldn't repress a smile at that thought. 'For me it was something beautiful. And I'll remember it even more happily because I think that, in your heart, you feel the same.'

I thought – *What?!* – but for some reason I couldn't find any coherent words with which to rebut that.

We were back a moment later. Lunch was ready, and all was bustle and kissing, and over lunch the story of the adventure got told with numerous action replays and minor disagreements about details, though of course the *chambre des pinsons* got no more than a passing mention, and the story came to an end some time before the bedroom door was finally shut for the night. After lunch, because everything was running late, it was already time to leave for the station, me carrying my overnight bag in one hand and my hare (mercifully skinned and eviscerated, and wrapped in newspaper for coolness) in the other. It was not for the first time, as I sat opposite Régine on the train, that I found difficulty in meeting her trusting brown eyes.

We said our *au revoirs* at the corner of the rue des Archives, and Fabrice took custody of the hare. He'd cook it for us and selected friends on Tuesday night, he said. I thought, how difficult it was to give yourself a break from people. You always seemed to end up inextricably entangled with them by the most trivial of connections: a bloody hare, for instance, or a pair of socks.

I dumped my bag at home and had a shower. It was my second one that day, but I took it for reasons that had nothing to do with physical cleanliness. Then I went out for a walk. I'd found the inside of my flat oppressive.

But I didn't feel much better when I got outside. It was that special period of Sunday afternoon that strikes even the bravest and best-fed as cheerless: the rapture of Friday evening a distant memory, the weekend tilting inexorably towards Monday morning. I'd once thought this melancholy time a peculiarly British phenomenon but my new life abroad was teaching me that this was not so. Sunday afternoon could be as bleak in Paris as in Northampton.

The quays of the Seine were busy with well-dressed strollers examining the second-hand bookstalls. Half Paris seemed to take its Sunday constitutional here, browsing among engravings and books that nobody ever seemed to buy. They probably came to see and to be seen, though they hardly ever seemed to run into anybody they knew. I crossed the Pont Neuf. The sunshine that had blessed the morning in Alsace had not followed the train to Paris, and the Seine ran past greyly with just a few glints of quicksilver to redeem its surface from total monochrome. The plane trees were now almost fully out along its banks, though the sun was not yet strong enough to produce the dappled shade that was the speciality of the place in summer. I turned away from the bridge into the Place Dauphine and there – coming straight towards me as if to defy the rule that you never ran into anyone you knew – was Joe.

I found myself wishing Joe had given me another twenty-four hours, just this once, to compose myself and collect my thoughts after the earth-shaking events of the last twenty-four. Still, I managed to tune my thoughts in to another wavelength and, remembering that Joe would normally be spending his weekends with Antoine these days, asked him what he was doing out and about on his own.

'Looking for you,' said Joe. 'I tried your bell, then the Horseshoe, then I called by the Figeac and had a coffee. You weren't there.' He paused before adding, 'But I guess you knew that. Seriously though,' he went on, 'Antoine's spending the weekend with his mother – that's why I'm on my own.'

'And the reason I wasn't in was that I've just come back from Alsace where I was spending the weekend, as you've probably forgotten.'

We began to drift along the quai des Orfèvres without thinking. Joe asked for an account of my weekend and, glad of the rehearsal opportunity that lunch with Fabrice's family had provided, I gave him the expurgated version. Nevertheless, Joe had enough prior information to add the one question that would not have occurred to anyone around the lunch table. 'God, quite an adventure. And you ending up alone with Fabrice for the night after all. Was there no...?' He let his expressive face provide the end of the question.

I didn't lie exactly. I think I set my jaw rather firmly. I said, 'Fabrice knows where I stand now,' in a rather grim tone of voice.

Joe said, rather feelingly, 'Poor Fabrice.' We continued to wander around the Ile de la Cité. Then Joe suddenly announced, 'We're thinking of getting a flat together.'

I had to think for a moment. Then I got there. 'We meaning Antoine and Joe, or we meaning Joe?'

'We, plural, but I take your point. It is me that's pushing for it. He has a few reservations.'

'I can imagine he has. He's, what, nineteen?'

Joe nodded.

'And you?'

'Twenty-six,' said Joe. 'One year younger than you.'

'How did you know that?'

'I didn't. It was an inspired guess; they're a speciality of mine. But I don't think his reservations are about me. At least, if what he says is true. He says he's concerned about the hard world outside. Parental expectations, pressures from friends, people at work. It's daunting.' Joe stopped a second, then resumed. 'I think I'm sure of him. I'm sure I'm sure. And yet, supposing he's just advancing those reasons so as not to hurt me?'

'Joe,' I said gently, 'I don't want to say anything unpopular but how can you really be sure with a boy of nineteen?'

'How is anyone sure of anything? If I tell you he loves me you have every reason to take that with a pinch of salt. It's only an inspired guess at this stage, after all. But then....'

Something rather obvious struck me. I said, 'Don't you think it's about time you introduced us? If I'd actually met him our discussion could perhaps become a little bit less abstract.'

Joe relaxed visibly. 'That's what I'd hoped you'd say. I'd been kind of putting off suggesting it myself.'

'Why on earth?'

'I'd have been hurt if you'd said you didn't want to meet him. Guess I still thought you disapproved of him in some way.'

'Just because I don't like men to make passes at me doesn't mean I disapprove of people being gay. But...'

'But what?'

'I don't want to sound stupid. But it's not being hurt by me that you need to worry about. Do you see?'

*

Much later that evening I sat on the end of my bed, just before I got into it, trying to make sense of the weekend's events with a little help from Beethoven. My curtains were open and I looked up suddenly when the familiar yellow light was switched on among the mansards opposite. I rubbed my still numb outer toes just as Fabrice had done that morning. I'd had some difficulty getting the socks off and wondered how I'd manage in the morning. Fabrice would not be there to help me, I thought absently. Then I realised with the sharp panic that comes with unwelcome new self-knowledge that a part of me wished he could be.

FOURTEEN

Joe had told me to come to a café called the Kabylie. It was near the place de la République. Joe and Antoine used it because no-one either of them knew frequented it. I found it eventually. There was a distinctly non-European feel to the place. The menu in the window strongly evoked North Africa and to judge by appearances – there being nothing else to go on, as Oscar Wilde said – so did the clientèle and staff. I was punctual but there was no sign of Joe or Antoine. Then a thought struck me. I looked around me. Joe had never said that Antoine was North African but he hadn't said he wasn't. A little self-consciously I leaned on the brightly polished copper counter and ordered myself a pastis. The hour for beer – as Jean-Jacques would have said – was past.

A few minutes went by and then a young European entered. He was of medium height and build, poised but unmannered in his movements and trimly dressed: his trousers were neatly pressed, his shoes polished. Straight brown hair was thick but kempt. His face tended towards the triangular but the features were perfectly proportioned. If the hazel eyes were on the large side they were at least supported by strong cheekbones and set off by lashes of a good length. The overall effect was of a normality so intense as to be striking. I wasn't sure whether the newcomer would have stood out in a crowd of his own age and race. Yet in his present setting he shone like a beacon. I had no doubt whatever that this was Antoine.

The guy caught sight of me and came up to me at once. His expression was grave; it flickered rather than smiled when he extended his hand and said – a French Stanley meeting a latter-day Livingstone – *'Peter, je suppose.'*

Ten more minutes passed and there was still no sign of Joe. 'Perhaps it's deliberate,' suggested Antoine, 'and he wants us to get to know each other at first without him.' We were relaxed together now and talking easily. Antoine sipped an orange juice while I nursed my pastis; the contrast made me feel uncomfortably old: at the same time decadent and *démodé*.

'Do you know many of Joe's friends?' I asked Antoine.

'One or two. He doesn't have all that many. You're the one he wanted me to meet especially. He said I'd find you interesting.'

There was a gravity, an earnestness about Antoine that I found inexplicably moving. He expressed himself soberly and intelligently, choosing his words with care. But by now I had discovered something else. Antoine possessed a characteristic not uncommon among the French. A face that was not given to smiling from force of habit would suddenly open into a spontaneous smile that dazzled with unlooked-for intensity and warmth. It was rather like the way some sober suited moths can spread dark wings to reveal beneath a blaze of colour and pure light.

At this point we were joined by one of those people encountered in bars who are called either characters or nuisances, depending on your point of view. This one, though dark-skinned, was not North African. That was apparent as soon as he opened his mouth. He came from Corsica, Antoine said.

'What's he saying?' I had to ask.

Antoine translated into a French that I could understand. 'He says it's good to see some real French people in here for a change. (He includes you in that. Appearances are a strange thing, *n'est-ce pas*?) That and *Vive Monsieur Le Pen*.'

'I see. Why does he use an Algerian bar, then? Do you know him?'

'By sight only,' said Antoine. 'It's the first time he's spoken to me.'

'Algerians?' said the other, older, man. 'Five of them set on me during the war.' He unrolled sleeves, showed scars, while Antoine relayed me the information. 'Don't talk to me about Algerians. And can I get a war pension? *Merde*.' He produced from his wallet a whole sheaf of letters in courteous bureaucratic French from various government departments, each one promising to refer his case to another one. He summoned the *patron* and ordered a pastis for himself and, refusing to take no for an answer, refills for Antoine and myself. 'Arabs,' he said, indicating the *patron*. 'All over here now. They're everywhere.'

Monsieur le Patron, who introduced himself to us two newcomers as Momo, took this in his stride and laughed.

Unlike Antoine he had a smile as ready as the Cheshire Cat's and when he laughed it became positively dazzling. 'One day,' he said, 'Corsica may be independent too. Then he …' he indicated the war veteran, 'He can be an immigrant like me.' Evidently this was as much of a ritual as the sparring of Carlos and Nico in the Horseshoe.

At that moment Joe arrived. 'What kept you?' Antoine asked innocently.

'Sorry.' Joe shrugged, then sat down. He turned to me and with an eagerness that was childlike in its lack of tact said, 'Well, you've met. What do you think of him?'

'He talks as if he'd just bought a racehorse,' objected Antoine, 'and a deaf one at that.' He turned to Joe. 'If you must discuss me behind my back, at least try not to do it in front of me.'

In *esprit* they were well-matched, I thought.

Antoine turned to me. 'I understand American but I refuse to speak it. We French have a duty to resist all attempts at cultural imperialism.'

Joe laughed. 'He's just afraid of making silly mistakes, that's all. He speaks English perfectly well.'

'That's not the point at all,' Antoine protested. 'If I give way now, where will France and the French be in forty years' time?'

'You do take a long view of things...' I began.

'For one so young,' Antoine finished the sentence for me. 'Yes. I think one should.'

'Come on,' said Joe. 'Let's go eat.'

It was only after we got to Joe's flat, when Antoine disappeared to the *toilettes* – which are always plural in French, be they never so humble – that we had a brief opportunity to talk about him, as he had instructed, behind his back. 'He's not quite what I imagined a nineteen-year-old baker's boy would be like,' I said.

'Exactly,' said Joe. 'He's not. Perhaps you can begin to see…'

'Perhaps I can.'

'It's spaghetti Bolognese by the way, because I'm the chef. At least I am tonight. Antoine's a far better cook than me and I could have asked him but tonight it didn't seem right. He likes my spaghetti anyway. Cultural imperialism with an Italian flavour doesn't seem to hurt so much. Anyway, about you for a bit,' Joe changed the subject. 'In Paris for two months and more – *en plus*, it's the spring – and there's no girl on your arm yet.'

That rather shook me. 'I suppose I haven't got round to it yet,' I said uncomfortably. 'Perhaps I'm fussy.' I wasn't happy about the change of subject. The difficulties I'd had trying to get my socks on this morning were fresh in my mind.

'But Peter, this is Paris! Just look around you. There's no possible excuse. It might be different in Timbuctoo where there's nothing but camels, but here...!' He gestured up and down the room as if to indicate that the whole delightful range of French womanhood was here on parade.

'I didn't know you were such an expert on the subject.'

'I may be gay but that doesn't make you blind, whatever they may have told you at school. What about that nice girl in the Figeac?'

Another shock. Did he mean... 'Françoise?'

'No of course not. I mean the waitress, Marianne.'

Well, it was good that he hadn't meant Françoise. But even so... 'Marianne does just happen to be attached, you know. She lives in the 5-ième with a guy you said would probably want to kill Dominique. Remember?'

'Lived with a guy. She doesn't now.'

'Come again?'

'She threw him out. She's a free woman.'

'Where the hell did you get hold of that? I didn't know anything about it.' I felt a bit put out. I thought I was the one who knew all the Figeac gossip.

Apparently not. Joe said, 'Madame Touret told me yesterday. I told you I went in for a coffee when I was looking for you. I naturally asked after Marianne – who was not on duty – and that was what Madame Touret said. But don't worry, my little concierge, you're not really behind with the news. It only happened on Saturday night.'

I said, 'Marianne's a lovely girl, I know, but to tell the honest truth I haven't taken too much interest since Becky and I split up.' I mugged a self-deprecating grimace. At least I tried to. 'I guess I'm a bit slow at getting things together again.' I was appalled at myself: appalled by the brazen lie that underpinned this rickety superstructure of half-truth.

'It isn't surprising,' said Joe, after a thoughtful pause. 'Although it is a bit different from my own experience. After Chris left me I wanted everything I saw. Fortunately I didn't always get it. Otherwise you can imagine where I'd be now. Anyway, it just goes to show how different people are.'

I was relieved that Antoine chose that moment to return to the room.

Joe's flat was just the same cramped, homely kind of space that I had, high up under the roof of a large *immeuble:* a combined office and apartment block. Unlike in mine, though, the kitchen was some way along the corridor and so I was left alone with Antoine while Joe put finishing touches to the meal. I broached the subject that had been troubling Joe. I was fairly sure that Joe wanted me to and had invited me this evening partly with this purpose in mind. I said, 'When are you two going to get a place together?'

Antoine didn't smile as he considered his reply. 'I

don't know,' he said. 'I'm not even sure it'll be possible.'

'I understand,' I said. 'It is a bit soon to commit yourself to a relationship, I suppose. Nineteen is young to make a final decision about something so important. Perhaps it's a time for trying out different things, experimenting, if you like, before finally settling down. Joe's a great guy but I respect your caution. After all, you don't know who you're going to meet.'

'If you think you understand,' said Antoine rather frostily, 'you couldn't be much more wrong. My hesitation about sharing a flat with Joe has nothing to do with our relationship – about which I have no uncertainties – and everything to do with my family situation: something I don't want to bore you with the details of. Just let me say that things are not good between my mother and my father. A move like that could overturn the whole wagon of apples – is that really what you say in English? – and my mother would get hurt more than she already has been.' He went on,

'Concerning relationships in general, you may be older than me and more wise but when you talk the way you did just now I think you may be talking about your own experience, not mine. You tell me I don't know who I'm going to meet. Well, that's certainly true. But at least I do know who I have met and it's just possible that in spite of your years and experience you don't. You tell me that nineteen is an age more for experiment than for commitment and though you were too polite to remind me directly that for some young people homosexuality may be a passing phase, you hinted it all the same.'

He got up from his chair and moved to the window, looking out of it while he continued his speech. The fluency of it and the passion that clearly underlay its measured delivery were startling, especially in combination with his youthful appearance. I guessed the speech had been delivered before; either that or it was being rehearsed for a bigger occasion.

'When I think about commitment I think about some stories from the past where people who didn't share their government's or their church's views had to set sail for countries they'd hardly heard of, that scarcely existed, that they might not even reach. Perhaps only the lucky ones could get a ticket. But suppose you said to those lucky ones, 'Oh come on, think about it. You have a ticket to a place nobody's returned from, your voyage will be hell and you might in any case end up at the bottom of the sea. And if you reach your promised land it may turn out to be just a desert. Change your mind; don't go.' How do you think those people would reply? 'Like hell I'll change my mind,' they'd say. 'Like hell, because I've had the luck to get a ticket.''

He turned his back to the window and faced me. 'That is what I'm saying to you. I have my ticket: that's Joe and my love for him. I'm not going to hand that back for anything or for anyone. Do you understand?'

'Yes,' I said, 'I think perhaps I do.' I felt as though Antoine had hit me over the head with a very large heavy object. The French word for this is *matraqué*. I felt flattened.

I marshalled my thoughts. After a moment or two I realised what I had to say. I discovered, if you like, the purpose of my visit. 'If you feel that strongly, then make the move and get a flat with him. Do it soon. If you make that your aim the rest will take care of itself. For you it's the only thing to do.'

'I'll consider it carefully,' said Antoine.

After the meal Antoine got up to go. I was a bit surprised. I'd imagined I'd be the first to depart, leaving the lovers together. 'I have a very early start tomorrow,' Antoine explained. 'In any case,' he added candidly, 'you'll want to talk about me. Tomorrow I can talk to Joe about you.'

'Well?' said Joe when he had gone.

The words popped out before I'd had time to choose them. 'He's beautiful,' I said.

FIFTEEN

Joe was invited to come and share the hare dinner. Antoine was working that evening and in any case Fabrice and Régine didn't know of his existence and so didn't realise that in entertaining Joe they would be entertaining not a whole single person but one half of a couple. Joe asked me quite innocently, why not ask Marianne? I'd said it was rather short notice for her as she would have to ask for a night off. The reality was more complicated than that. I couldn't go into that with Joe, though. I didn't know what the reality was. I just knew there was this ongoing difficulty with putting on my socks without Fabrice.

But the hare would make a vast main course for just four people and so Fabrice suggested we invite Françoise. But Régine said Françoise wouldn't want to come without the dodgy Portuguese guy, and nobody wanted to invite him. In the end we decided to invite Jeannette and Denis, the other couple who had shared the big table at the Figeac on my first evening in Paris.

With everyone coming from different directions, and Joe in particular not knowing where Fabrice and Régine lived, we met to begin with at the Little Horseshoe and then walked round the block to their apartment once we had all arrived. This meant that everyone at the bar knew exactly who was dining where, and that everyone at the Figeac would also know within about ten minutes. That was the way life was lived in the Marais. I was getting used to it.

There were oysters to begin the meal. April being the last month with an R in it before September, it seemed only common sense to take advantage of them before the breeding season kicked them into touch. Denis volunteered for the martyr's role of opening them alone in the kitchen while everyone else chatted over an aperitif in *le living*, and he did this with a good deal of off-stage swearing, which helped to maintain his presence in the social gathering despite his being the other side of the open door.

I was conscious the whole time, as we sat sipping Pineau de Charentes and chatting politely about nothing very much, of my physical position in relation to Fabrice, to say nothing of the intermittent eye contact between us. Now we were sitting on opposite sofas, feet stretched out towards the middle of the room at about a hundred and fifty degrees to each other, our feet about a metre apart. Now, when Fabrice had gone to check on Denis in the kitchen and given him some moral support in the shape of a topped-up glass, and was back with a bowl of *amuse-gueules,* he stood for a moment near my shoulder. And I was astonished to find that I could smell him. Not at all in an unpleasant way. Yet under the masks of after-shave, clean clothes, deodorant and soap, there was the unmistakeable scent that was Fabrice: a scent unknown to me and undetectable a week ago but now as familiar to me as my own. And was it my imagination or could I actually feel his body heat as well?

Then Fabrice was back on his sofa. Catching my eye a moment. Settled again, legs outstretched, this time at one hundred and eighty degrees, less than a metre between our two pairs of shoes. I stole a look around the room. I hadn't memorised anyone else's position in the same way; those spatial details hadn't impinged on me at all.

At the table in the dining-room that was also the kitchen, I sat in the same seat as I'd done on my only other visit, my *à deux* Sunday lunch with Fabrice back in February. As then, Fabrice sat opposite me; meanwhile the others seemed disposed at random around the table – Régine, the lady of the house, seeming no more fixed in her orbit than Joe, Denis or Jeannette in theirs – like the positions of the planets before the invention of astronomy allotted them their spheres.

The hare had been cooking by itself in the oven, in a quantity of red wine and with shallots, juniper berries, orange peel and a bay leaf, tantalising us with its aromas, and Fabrice only had to leave the table for a few minutes after the oysters had been lip-smackingly despatched, to prepare its single, plain accompaniment: gnocchi. Even that slightly fiddly task he carried out with effortless aplomb, taking the previously shaped miniature potato dumplings from their film-wrapped inertia in the fridge and dropping them into boiling water, waiting carefully till each one floated before skimming it out with a slotted spoon.

Of course the weekend in Alsace which had produced the hare that was the focus of this gathering had to be hauled into the conversation, and its adventures rehearsed yet again in detail, for the benefit of Denis and Jeannette. Fabrice asked me, with a hint of mischief in his blue eyes, if my feet were getting their sensation back. Wanting to kick him under the table, but resisting the impulse in case Fabrice should mistake it for a gesture of affection, I said seriously that the feeling had returned to all but the tips of my two smallest toes, that they still tended to poke sideways into my socks when I was dressing myself but that, by the careful deployment of a new technique that involved both hands, I was now able to manage the daily problem quite easily. All of this was new to Joe, and he became quite curious on the subject. I was well aware that his real curiosity was as to why I'd omitted this detail, about which Fabrice clearly had intimate knowledge, from the account of the weekend that I'd given him.

In an effort to divert the company's interest away from the subject of my feet I finally said to Joe, 'What a pity Antoine couldn't make it.' And of course everyone wanted to know who Antoine was, to which Joe calmly replied, using the English words, that he was his 'Significant Lover,' which everybody understood, even if only I and Fabrice really got the joke. Joe was making a public declaration of his sexual orientation: no French female ever bore the name Antoine, but in the company then present this created no frisson or awkwardness at all. People simply asked the usual interested but not too probing dinner party questions about who and where Antoine was.

But if the heterosexual members of the gathering

accepted the entrance of Antoine into the conversation as a matter of course, this was far from being the case along the axis between Fabrice and myself. I had a sudden vivid impression of this axis as something tangible connecting us, like a line of fishing nylon which, given a tweak by a third party, caused us both to twitch comically in response. Our eyes met, but that was only part of it. It seemed to me then that the things between us – what we had done together; and my rather hopeless wish that history could go into rewind and return us to the less complicated relationship of earlier times – must be visible to everyone else in the room.

Conversation had moved on. I came back to it with a start. 'For about three weeks,' Régine was saying. 'Terribly short notice. But then we're back for the summer.' Fabrice's bank, it seemed, had that day summoned him to Strasbourg for a short spell at headquarters. Régine would be going with him; she was owed some holiday. And when would they be going, I asked?

I thought, thank God for this. My feelings for Fabrice were now both complex and intense. I thought we both perhaps needed a space of time apart that would act as a fire-break between us. The day after tomorrow, Régine said. A quick drink in the Little Horseshoe tomorrow evening, because there would be packing to do, and then *au revoir* till next month.

When the party broke up finally, after quite a few bottles had crashed into the kitchen waste-bin, goodnight kisses were exchanged freely by everyone: all the men kissed each other, even Denis and Joe, who had never met before tonight. Somehow I was the last to depart from the head of the stairs; I kissed Régine, who then moved back inside the flat, and I was left with Fabrice, who had once stood on this very spot and told me not to be so British. We exchanged the polite formal kiss and then, without thinking, reinforced it with a hug, and the hug grew extended in time until it more resembled a cuddle. And though this evening we had both kept our promise not to refer ever again to our sexual adventure, I found that the memory was engraved into our embrace. I found it written there in indelible script, recorded by voices that could never be erased. And having once felt the reality of Fabrice's warm nakedness against my own bare skin, I discovered that I could feel it again now, even through our two sets of clothes, and I guessed that whenever I touched Fabrice physically in the future, were it only in a handshake, I always would do. Thank God he was going away for a few weeks.

'C'mon, Peter. You coming or what?' Joe's voice from the bottom of the stairwell recalled me to myself

SIXTEEN

Paris. April. 1987.

The night was warm. I dressed in my oldest, ripped-knee jeans and threw on my leather jacket, lined with fleece. I wore that next to my skin. Just like the jeans. No underpants. Trainers without socks. Nothing else.

I turned down the rue des Archives beneath the yellow stars of its street-lamps. Turned right along the quays. Quai de Gesvres, quai Mégisserie, quai du Louvre, quai des Tuileries... Does every bisexual man come here in the end?

Where it became dark, beneath the deep trees, there began the sounds, the rustles, the whispers, the occasional moan, of men enjoying sex. They were invisible in the darkness, their exact location betrayed occasionally by the dim red fireflies that were cigarettes.

I'd bought my own packet of Gitanes for once. I smoked one as I walked hesitatingly along. I chose a place, a dark place midway between two lamp posts, and stopped on the path where I was.

A guy came out of nowhere. He was Asian looking. About my age. About my size. His face was beautiful – like a Siamese cat's. 'T'as un clops pour moi?' he said. I let him pull one out of my packet. He put it in his mouth and lit it from the end of mine. Then with his free hand he started to fumble with the buckle of my belt.

I jerked my head towards the shadowy trees. 'Là-bas,' I said.

Now we were in shade and shadow, looking outward towards the light of the river-bank night. We dropped our half-smoked Gitanes and ground them out. I felt safe and cocooned here as we groped each other's jeans down and released each other's confined hard cocks. Standing face to face we started to wank each other. He bobbed down after a moment and took my prick in his mouth. Then he bobbed back up again and gave me a grin I didn't expect. That prompted me to crouch down and return his compliment. We finished each other off by hand, standing at an angle to each other so as not to mess each other's clothes. After we'd both come – almost simultaneously – we put a cautious arm around each other's shoulder. Then to my surprise he kissed me almost passionately for a second, before we parted, disappearing into each other's darknesses, without saying goodnight.

*

I hadn't said a proper au revoir to Fabrice. There had been that quick farewell drink at the Little Horseshoe the night after the dinner party with the hare. But Régine had been there, and Joe, and Françoise... We hadn't had a moment to exchange a private word – although we'd exchanged a few private if difficult-to-read looks. We'd shaken hands on the pavement. Straight men in Paris often kiss on these occasions. But that day Fabrice and I did not.

I busied myself with writing. I burnt with a hard and gem-like flame. I still went to the Figeac. I walked and talked with Joe. But somehow nothing was the same. Yet time passed quickly. It was almost a shock when the month of May arrived, with weather good enough to hint at a hot continental summer to come, and a telephone call from Margueritte – she was in Barcelona – to say she was coming to Paris to collect my rent.

*

I got a phone call unexpectedly from a woman friend. I'd been at university with Helen, and despite her marriage soon afterwards to a man called James we'd kept in touch ever since. She was in Paris for two days. James was at a conference; she had come along for the ride. Could we meet for dinner tonight? I said yes, of course and told them how to find the Figeac. I hadn't been there for about a week.

The Figeac appealed to Helen and her husband as I hope it would. The birds sang from the window recesses as we entered, for the evenings were light now, and Madame Touret welcomed us, more calculatingly, with an aperitif on the house. She was once more on bar duty. Marianne had gone to a new job nearer to where she lived and a suitable replacement had not been found. I guessed that Madame Touret was very particular in her requirements. Marianne was greatly missed.

Jean-Jacques volunteered a perfunctory handshake. He did not eat, he said. Then he returned to *Libération*. Dominique proved more entertaining. He arrived at the same time as our *entrecôte aux cèpes* and joined us at our table without being asked, as a child might.

'Have you heard about Françoise?' he asked me at once, with barely a nod to acknowledge the presence of the others. He did not wait for an answer either. 'The Portuguese guy has taken over her shop. Tells her how to run the business, insists on serving the customers, ordering the staff around...'

'Can't she stop him?' I asked.

'He won't take no for an answer. Difficult to forbid someone your shop when he's already in your bed. She'd have to change the locks or go to the police. She doesn't want to do that, she says. She's decided she's in love with him and that's that. She'd rather not have him as a business partner, that's all.'

'Difficult.' I wasn't sure how I could include my guests in the conversation. Or if I should.

'You know he has a prison record?' Dominique continued, still completely ignoring my friends.

'Luisa did say something of the sort, yes. Though I don't know...'

'For forging cheques,' Dominique said.

'*Mon dieu!* Does Françoise know?' I felt this keenly. I'd decided weeks ago not to tell Françoise what Luisa had said about her cousin. Maybe I'd called it wrong.

'People have tried to tell her. She doesn't listen.'

I felt slightly better. I had to introduce Dominique now if he was going to stay. Helen and James were looking bewildered. Helen had been trying gamely to follow the story, James losing the battle with the language. I attempted a brief résumé in English.

'A typical Parisian set-up?' James asked.

'They're not Parisians,' I said, as if in mitigation. 'Françoise was born here but her parents were provincials. And the Portuguese, of course, is Portuguese. To tell the truth, I haven't met a real Parisian yet. Unless Dominique...?' I turned to him. 'Where are you from originally, Dominique?'

'Look at me,' he answered. His eyes and complexion clearly said south. 'My father came from the department of the Lot. Your friends?'

'From Britain,' I said. 'Helen's a part of my past. We were at university together. James is her husband.'

'Ah, the past,' said Dominique, seizing on the word that interested him most, like a philosopher who has heard a much misunderstood concept dropped into a casual conversation. 'The past is life's capital investment. Invested well it will pay a good dividend. The dividend is your future.'

I translated.

'I see,' said James, frowning a bit. 'Er ... Should we offer him a glass of wine?'

'If you look at the bottle,' said his wife, 'you'll see from the level that your offer's been accepted in advance.' She addressed Dominique, bravely attempting French. 'What do you mean about investing the past wisely? Money can be moved from one place to another in order to … er...'

'Attract a better return,' I helped out.

'But the past is immutable, surely. I don't see what you can 'do' with it.'

'I think it can be changed,' answered Dominique, 'though it's only my opinion. And you can do almost anything with it in your head.'

After a moment's thought we discovered we could all agree with the last point at least.

Helen reverted to English for her next question – which I then translated for Dominique. 'When you 'change the past' as you say you do, is it a once for all affair or something that offers multiple chances? I mean chances in careers, with relationships, chances to be happy. If this opportunity you speak of was a cherry, in other words, dangling in front of you, would you be allowed only one attempt to bite it from the stalk or could you try again?'

I put the all too graphic image into French with some apprehension. I was sure Dominique would choke on his wine.

He did not. 'It's like this,' he said. 'Imagine the sky at

night. How many stars do you see? A million? A hundred million? No, an infinite number, small and large, bright and veiled, near and far. And can you have them all? Do you suppose that each single one was put there just for you? No, of course not. But suppose on the other hand that only one is there for you. Only one in all infinity. That must be nonsense too. Life couldn't be so ungenerous as to offer only one chance. That's what I think And, for me especially, I hope.'

'Why for you in particular?' Helen asked.

'I tried to kill the woman I loved,' he said simply. 'Luckily she's still alive.' He looked down as he said this and I braced myself for another emotional scene. But then Dominique's eyes lit on the wine bottle which was nearly empty, a discovery that shocked him into action: he went at once to the bar to negotiate for a replacement.

'Did he really try to kill his woman?' James asked in fascinated horror.

'Up to a point,' I said. 'Up to a point.'

Just then someone else came in and looked around a little uncertainly. With a start I found myself greeting Fabrice, who smiled when he saw me and came over. He was wearing a blue denim jacket of the same type that I was wearing this evening, or had been before I'd hooked it over the back of my restaurant chair. 'I hardly recognized you,' I said. 'This bohemian outfit.' I fingered Fabrice's jacket and gestured towards his jeans.

Fabrice looked at the table and at my guests. Might he... ?

Might he not. I introduced him, invited him to sit down, and he joined us just as Dominique, with immaculate timing, returned with a new bottle of wine. I couldn't believe Fabrice's three weeks in Strasbourg were up so soon. I'd deliberately not allowed myself to count the days. But where was Régine?

If it wasn't one thing it was another, Fabrice explained. He took his jacket off, as if in imitation of my shirt-sleeved state. No sooner had they got back, he said, than she'd been called away by her own TV company bosses. They were making a series of programmes over the border in Italy; there was some financial stuff to negotiate and she'd been needed there too. She sent her love and was sorry she hadn't had time to... I waved her apologies away. I was pleased to be able to show off the most presentable of my new friends to Helen. Better than letting her think I only socialised with the likes of Dominique. And, complications notwithstanding, it was more than just agreeable to see Fabrice again.

Soon it was late. I walked back with Helen and James to their hotel, agreed to meet Helen the following afternoon while James was at his conference, and said goodnight. Then I walked home. Buzzing the right code buttons got me through the outer doors, and the doors at the foot of my staircase were open as usual. But to get into my apartment I needed my key. I felt for it in the pocket of my jacket, which I was carrying over my shoulder. It wasn't there. I placed the jacket on the baluster head and ferreted through all the pockets. The situation quickly became clear, even before I'd confirmed it by fishing out an unfamiliar hanky and a wallet with Fabrice's name in it. Of Fabrice's keys there was no sign. I guessed he kept them in his trouser pocket or clipped to his belt, so he would have arrived home without missing them or – presumably – needing his wallet. Fabrice was all right for now, though he wouldn't be when he wanted money in the morning. I, on the other hand...

I returned to the Figeac. I got there just in time: in a few minutes the doors would be locked. René was stacking chairs on tables while the new waitress swept beneath them, and Madame Touret was busy tidying up in the kitchen. She was just calling to her son to ask if the till was done.

No, my jacket wasn't there. Did they remember if Fabrice had left wearing one? Carrying one? They couldn't swear to it, but they thought so. In any case, I'd have to go round to Fabrice's flat now to return his wallet. They wished me *bon courage*.

Unlike Dominique, I didn't carry all the door-codes of the *quartier* in my head, so I had to press Fabrice's bell and wait on the pavement for an answer. It took some time to come. For an anxious moment it went through my mind that, though Fabrice had said Régine was away, he hadn't actually said that he would be on his own. He might be ... well, I didn't want to think about that. Fabrice's private life was his own. Nothing to do with me. I was simply coming to return a jacket and, I hoped, get mine back.

Fabrice's voice came through crackle. *'C'est qui?'*

'C'est moi: Pierre.' Why I gave my name in French I had no idea.

'Peter, you crazy boy.' Fabrice's laugh too came through the crackle. 'Come up.'

When I got to the stair-head, there was Fabrice, waiting for me, leaning over the banisters. He was wearing a towelling bathrobe. Blue. Like his eyes. Like mine.

'I think you've got my jacket,' I said as I made my way up the last flight 'This one's certainly yours.'

'You're kidding,' said Fabrice. We both walked into the apartment. Fabrice went at once to where he'd hung the garment he'd worn back from the Figeac. He looked at it briefly, dipped a hand into a pocket, said, 'Oh sorry,' as soon as his fingers encountered unfamiliar objects, and then almost handed it back to me. But he stopped in mid-movement and said, suddenly regressing, both in voice and in facial expression, to the gauche and timid teenager he might have been twelve years before, 'Would you like a night-cap?'

'Um, no, really. I only came about the jacket.' But something in my voice betrayed me. Fabrice put his jacket-encumbered arms around me, and I realised as I relaxed into that warm embrace and returned it with interest, that not only would I not be needing my door-keys tonight but that this was how I'd unconsciously been wanting this reunion evening to end for the last three weeks.

Anthony McDonald

SEVENTEEN

Helen and I were on the terrace of Les Deux Magots, drinking two of the most expensive cups of coffee we'd ever tasted. In return we had the satisfaction of knowing that Sartre and his circle had passed their days in the same spot, though presumably drinking more cheaply. A notice on the wall forbade you to spin out your *consommation* for more than an hour without ordering a replacement. It would only be possible now to write post-cards here or to dash off a sonnet. To sit here and embark on any larger literary form would take the resources of a millionaire.

I stood up. 'Come on. Let's walk.' We were in the middle of a ramble round the Quartier Latin. We threaded through tiny streets little longer than their width towards the rue St. André des Arts, a huddle of old eccentric houses and deeply shaded doorways. Already, though it was only May, the street was thronged with tourists. I pointed down the rue Mazet to the place where Doctor Guillotin had honed his invention by experiments on sheep. Then we emerged onto the quai des Malaquais opposite the Louvre and, as a good guide must, I indicated the house where Voltaire had sharpened his barbed pen. Barges ploughed up and down the Seine in front of us. Across the river the Louvre's long southern wall extended in an endless repetition of identical pillars and windows. It looked like an illustration of the idea of infinity. The vista eventually lost itself in a green and white fur of trees: horse chestnuts at full candle-power in

The Paris Novel

the Tuileries gardens.

Under those lovely trees, in the darkness of the night, two weeks ago, I'd sucked a stranger's cock.

'How beautiful Paris is,' said Helen.

'Yes,' I said, 'but sometimes I think it's only beautiful like dreams are beautiful.'

We turned our backs on the river and its monumental vistas and burrowed once more into the labyrinth of the Quartier Latin.

We came upon the place Furstenberg, a miniature square of brick and plane trees that opened out suddenly in our path. We sat down on a bench in its peaceful shade.

'It's good you're making friends here,' Helen said. 'I liked Dominique.' Then she shot me a very searching look. 'I especially liked Fabrice.'

I sometimes wondered if the things I didn't really know about myself were written on my forehead for everyone to read except me. I tried to shift the conversation – and my thoughts – away from Fabrice. I said, 'I have another friend I like lot. Name of Joe. American, male, sensitive, gay. He's recently got involved with a nineteen-year-old. He's decided – no, to be fair, they both have – that it's going to be the partnership of a lifetime. Of both their lifetimes.'

'Good for them,' said Helen staunchly. 'Will it work,

do you think?'

I said, 'Perhaps. I've met the kid. He's good, and sensible. In fact he has a kind of precocious wisdom that's a bit unsettling when you first encounter it. In a strange way he might be able to keep Joe's feet on the ground, if anyone can. Yes, it might work out. Look there.'

I had to interrupt myself. We'd wandered up the rue Bonaparte and I pointed down a side street to a white-fronted house over whose doorway sprang a silver carved ram's head. 'That's the house where Oscar Wilde died,' I said. 'Hotel, I should say, because that's what it is and was even then. There was a problem with the bill. 'I'm dying as I've always lived,' he's supposed to have said. 'Beyond my means.' These days it's quite an expensive hotel and sought after because of the connection. The bill has been paid with interest, as it were. Funny.'

'I hope they take all the proper precautions,' Helen said.

'The hotel?'

'Your two friends. You know. Don't die of ignorance and so on.' Helen turned to look at me. I must have turned colour. I felt faint. 'You OK?' she said.

I pulled myself together. 'Fine,' I said. 'Hey, look. Let's wander over to the Ile de St Louis. We can have an ice-cream at Berthillon's. Tell ourselves that summer's really here at last.'

The Paris Novel

*

Helen and James were going to the opera later and had invited me to go with them. I told Helen as I parted from her in their hotel doorway that I wouldn't be joining them and hoped they wouldn't mind. I'd join them for a drink before they left the following evening if that was all right.

I walked away. For a few moments I thought in desperation that I'd have to talk to Dominique. I'd say something like this. 'Look, I'm sorry to drop this on you, but you're the only person I know who ... I mean, perhaps you can advise me. A friend of mine who's bisexual is a little bit worried about, well, you know what. Because of something that happened to him recently. No, I don't know exactly what. He didn't tell me and I didn't ask. Well, I thought I could do him a favour, because, knowing you as I do, I thought you might know an address in Paris where I could ... I mean where he could... get some sort of a test, if you see what I mean...' Just running the speech in my head made me go hot and cold. Talking to Dominique was out of the question. And I certainly wasn't going to talk to Joe about this.

I made my way to the pavement outside the Little Horseshoe, ordered a beer and waited grimly for Fabrice to appear.

He did. He came sauntering down the street from the Métro in the evening sunshine and looking as if life were the most uncomplicated business imaginable. 'Hi,' he said. 'Thought I might find you here.'

I said, 'Well, I didn't. I was supposed to be going to the opera tonight, if you remember, with Helen and James.'

He ignored my chilly tone and joined me at the table. 'People do change their plans, you know.'

I said, 'Not only that. I thought it might be better – for both of us – if we didn't see quite so much of each other for a bit.'

Fabrice hauled in a breath. 'I see.'

'Only, since last night I've realised there's a question I should have asked you. Look...' I looked around us. 'Can we do this bit in English?'

'Oh all right, mister,' Fabrice obliged at once. 'It's that serious, then?'

'I need to know if you … I mean, there's someone I know who … no, this is stupid … I mean, are you HIV positive? Or do you know, one way or the other?'

Fabrice smiled quickly, nervously, audibly. Then he looked serious again. 'OK. I understand. Because you found yourself last night on the … er … receiving end of something for the first time, you're now scared of receiving something else too. But you weren't too bothered about all that when you … you know, in the Chaffinch Bedroom.' It seemed strange to hear Fabrice translating even the *chambre des pinsons* into English.

The Paris Novel

'Yes, but...'

'Yes, but I'm labelled bisexual in your mind, and so therefore a whore and I probably sleep with everyone I meet, whereas you're the big tough, straight guy who never...'

'Fabrice, fuck you. Just shut up and give me an answer. If I've upset you I'll apologise after.'

Our conversation was being followed with rapt, if covert, attention by everyone else on the *terrasse*, the more so for its being conducted in English at an increasingly intense pianissimo.

Fabrice consented to answer my question. 'I had a scare myself once, like you did. I went to Belleville after the agonising time lapse and had a test done. I was negative. Now you can either believe me that I'm still clear – just like I trusted you that first time – or I can give you the address and, after a suitable interval you can go along yourself.'

Was that the moment when the domino tower I'd been building all my life inside me finally collapsed? Well, no, not all of it. Not then. But a good big part of it did. I was falling, deep inside myself, into something huge and new and terrifying. I found I wanted to hug Fabrice then and shower his face with a storm of kisses, but since we were sitting on the pavement outside the Horseshoe, I just looked across the table at him with eyes that swam suddenly with tears.

'I think,' said Fabrice, still in English, but with a catch

in his voice, 'that I should order us both a drink.'

I was heady with relief, stratospherically high, at what I saw as my second escape from a brush with death courtesy of Fabrice. I was high on other emotions too, but I hadn't had time to examine them yet. I accepted Fabrice's suggestion, a beer or two later, that we dine together at the Figeac and I put up no more than a token resistance at the end of the meal when Fabrice picked up the bill. After all, we both agreed, he was two years older, two inches taller, and worked for a merchant bank. Nor did my conscience veto the way in which the evening ended.

And the way that evening ended was to serve as a model for the nights which followed.

Paris. May. 1987.

Sometimes we smoke Gitanes in bed. I never before smoked with anyone in bed. The colour of his skin is special. Somewhere between the living breathing pink of herring roe and the cool depth of honey vanilla ice-cream. His penis is the most beautiful one I've ever seen. It's an inch longer then mine is. We measured them for fun one night. It's straight, and tapers very slightly towards the tip. Like me, he's uncircumcised. Like mine, the tip of it is not so much blue as pink.

He's tall. I'm smaller. But we have other things in common. We both have a sexy gap between our top front teeth. We have blond hair and blue eyes, both of us. We both have black eyebrows, eyelashes, beards – his in the form of a moustache only – and black body hair, including pubes.

His balls are the colour of milky coffee into which strawberry juice has been stirred.

Joining him in bed at night is like climbing into a warm bath. His muscles are firm yet yielding. They yield to me, that is.

I've never felt the way I do with him in bed with anyone before. Fucking him, being fucked by him, sucking, cock-stroking... It's never been that good with anyone in my life.

To get out of bed in the morning is a real wrench. The wonderful night turns to morning surreally, with him helping to get my frost-numbed toes into my socks.

*

Régine would not be back until the weekend, and meanwhile I took the opportunity to spend as much time as possible with her boyfriend. We tried out restaurants where we were still strangers, because there were limits to what even our acquaintances in the Marais might be expected to turn a blind eye to, and Fabrice took me to other places I might not have found on my own.

We went to hear Olivier Messiaen playing the organ at the Gregorian Mass in La Trinité, the white church with its sugar-sifter of a belfry that stands at the end of the rue Chaussée d'Antin. The great man did not accompany the choir, a lesser mortal saw to that, but his improvisatory voluntaries punctuated the service: the organ roared and thundered like the might of God, pleaded in the voices of suppliant sinners, resolved into a final harmony of merciful reconciliation, while Messiaen, the channel down which these revelations flowed, remained unseen and anonymous in the loft at the back of the echoing church.

Fabrice introduced me to a late night music bar called the Petit Piano Zinc – *'C'est gai mais ce n'est pas le ghetto,'* Fabrice explained – where I found myself welcomed (the next words are Fabrice's, not mine) as 'a highly attractive newcomer.' And at the end of the evening, always, pleasantly just a little bit drunk, we would fall into Fabrice's – I tried not to think, Fabrice and Régine's – double bed.

I was hitting the sack, night after night, with the male partner of a woman friend who had taken me on trust as the straight guy and honest friend of my own estimation. It was impossible to make any sense of this breathtaking departure from precedent and I soon gave up trying. I dealt with the situation at a purely practical level, withdrawing strategically as the weekend approached, leaving Fabrice to deal with his own conscience vis a vis Régine. Presumably he also changed the sheets. I didn't want to know. I met Régine and Fabrice together once during that weekend, quite casually, over dinner at the big table in the Figeac and found myself behaving with exactly the same practised insouciance – that of the habitual deceiver – that Fabrice had demonstrated in similar circumstances for as long as I'd known him.

Then the weekend ended. Régine went back to work again in Italy, and I moved back in with Fabrice.

Anthony McDonald

EIGHTEEN

Paris. June. 1987

The weather shifted gear from warm to hot. I bought a thermometer in Madame Almuslih's shop. She sold everything from olives to tin foil, from mouse-traps to figs. In Britain thermometers were marked in Fahrenheit as well as centigrade and I could register the centigrade figure mentally while feeling the temperature in Fahrenheit. That was something ingrained from childhood like manners and the language. (It's barely fifty, put a coat on. Or: What a scorcher, eighty-four in the shade.) In France I had to learn finally to feel in centigrade just as I had to think in French. (Trente degrés, parait-il! ... Tu rigoles. ... Faut croire!) I hung my new acquisition outside my window, an unravelled paper-clip serving as a hook to attach it to the louvred shutter, and day by day would mark the upward progress of its coloured liquid thread.

The working day finished in sunshine that still spoke of afternoon, not evening, and dusk was banished to bedtime – a time which had suddenly acquired a new intensity of meaning. Meanwhile the tentative street life of spring was giving way to the full-blooded version of summer. Doors and windows stood perpetually open while goods and salespeople seemed to cascade from the shops onto the pavement. The city was turning inside-out like a glove, its population permanently on show instead of behind shutters. Sitting outside the Horseshoe with

The Paris Novel

Fabrice it was possible to wave to, even talk with, Madame Touret if she happened to be taking the sun with customers outside the Figeac and, without moving, to relay news down to the café on the next corner if its importance warranted – though this responsibility more usually fell to Dominique than to me or Fabrice.

Swifts sliced the still air of the streets, manoeuvring like champion skaters, fast and black against the blue, their screams, the sound of old and ill-used brakes, making the sky shrill. Neighbours till now un-glimpsed appeared and disappeared at windows and on balconies all around like characters in an opera and, even if they did not sing, their conversations ricocheted just as energetically down the street, zigzagging from wall to wall. In more reflective moods they watered their plants – geraniums and bizzy-lizzies on every balcony in clusters of flame – and in watering them watered too the passers-by beneath, some of whom appreciated the cooling showers while some did not.

June was heralded by Margueritte d'Alabouvettes telephoning from Frankfurt. If I was short of French francs, she said, she would be equally happy with dollars or Deutschmarks. I said that francs would present no problem. My thermometer was nudging thirty-three.

*

That the gold-spangled cousin of my concierge Luisa was arrested and removed from the public eye came as a surprise to no-one although it made a good talking-point.

Interpol had been seeking him since he had escaped from prison in Portugal while awaiting trial for armed robbery. The day after I heard about this I saw Françoise dining alone at the Figeac, dressed in sober blue. I joined her for I was alone too. It was the weekend again and Régine was back once more with Fabrice. 'I heard the news,' I said. 'I'm really very sorry.'

Françoise stared at me with wide eyes that looked accustomed to tears. 'It makes no difference to me,' she said. 'I still love him. I'll find a way to join him when I can.'

I asked boldly, 'Yes, but does he love you?'

'That,' she said with a chilling fatalism, 'has nothing to do with anything.'

I thought about this later. If that was love, and I was prepared to take Françoise's word for it since I could think of no other explanation for her behaviour, then that was not quite the same as my relationship with Fabrice. I liked Fabrice a lot, no doubt about it. He was a good friend, with nice looks and a lovely personality. I also enjoyed sex with him, very much. But I told myself that that was that.

I reminded myself that lots of men experienced a homosexual phase in their teens. I'd never gone through this stage of development. Was it unreasonable to suppose that life didn't have to happen to everybody in the same order? Surely it was conceivable that Fabrice and I were belatedly going through something quite usual: an exploration, a voyage of self-discovery that many other people undertook rather earlier in life. With any luck, I hoped., we would return to our port of embarkation, safe and sound, wiser but with no harm done to our heterosexual credentials, as soon as Régine returned from Italy in about two weeks' time.

*

In Madame Almuslih's shop one day Fabrice and I were surprised to find our normal greeting returned by silence from her habitually cheerful children and by a very choked *bonjour* from the lady herself. We didn't ask then and there what the problem was; we asked Madame Touret a little later.

'But hadn't you heard, Peter? She has to leave. To sell the business.'

We looked at each other. 'But why?' said Fabrice. 'It's flourishing. I know she and the kids work like dingoes for it but she must be making a small fortune.'

'She has a big bill to pay. You know, I suppose, that her husband is serving a term for homicide?'

'I knew he was in prison for something,' Fabrice said and I added carelessly, 'It seems every trader in the *quartier* is in prison for one reason or another.'

'There are exceptions,' said Madame Touret tartly, but she quickly relaxed, having the opportunity that every gossip relishes of telling an old story to people who missed it the first time round. 'Monsieur Almuslih was attacked one night by an armed man while he sat alone at the cash-desk. He used the bread-knife to defend himself and killed him stone dead. Poor man.'

It was not clear which of the two men Madame Touret sympathised with. We nodded our agreement anyway.

'As it happened, the gun was a plastic toy.'

'Perhaps Monsieur Almuslih would have got off more lightly if he had been a Monsieur Dupont,' Fabrice suggested. 'French instead of Moroccan.'

Madame Touret looked shocked. 'You are surely not suggesting that there's one law for the French and another for immigrants?'

Fabrice backed down. 'I just thought it was a possibility.'

'Anyway,' Madame Touret went on, 'Madame Almuslih is legally responsible for the court's award to the dead man's family plus the costs. Even more unfortunate is that there was an invalid son and providing for him has turned out very expensive.'

'So she has to sell up?' I said.

'That's right.'

'And instead of being able to pay her way she'll be a charge on the state?'

'C'est ça.'

'But it's totally crazy,' said Fabrice.

'That's the law, it appears.' Madame Touret then looked at me. 'Is it so very different in England?'

I wasn't sure but I thought probably not.

Jean-Jacques joined us. He already knew the story. 'Is there nothing we can do?' I asked him.

'What do you suggest?' said Jean-Jacques. 'Pass a hat round the restaurant for the money? I fear such sums might be beyond our modest resources. (A kir, please, *Madame* ... *merçi*.) And yet, and yet, maybe there is something we could try. The gnawing of a mouse may rock mountains. The voice of a child may tell the emperor that he has no clothes.' He turned to Fabrice. 'You have access to word-processing machines, I suppose? Computers? Things like that?'

Fabrice said, yes, he did.

'Good,' said Jean-Jacques. 'I can have the text ready tomorrow.'

'The text of what?' I asked. The poet took a sip from the ruby-coloured depths of his glass and explained to us what he had in mind.

*

We 'pillars' of the Figeac took it in turns over the next few days to sit at an outdoor table with the petition that Fabrice had had beautifully typed at work, accosting every half familiar face that passed: 'Do you shop over there? Read this. Now sign.' Everyone did.

'Go for the foreigners too, Peter,' the poet urged. 'The more international the list looks the better.' He had made me put my own name and address first. 'What's your surname? Ferguson? *Ah, bon.* Smith would have been better. Still, nobody's perfect. And something like O'Shaughnessy might have frightened them off. The bureaucrat is a shy, wild creature. He needs to be stalked with care.'

Jean-Jacques's eloquent text took the form of an open letter to the President of the Republic. In it he stressed France's traditional hospitality towards its non-native population and the practical and humane reasons that argued the tempering of the law with the spirit of clemency. Copies were sent to all government departments, to the Hôtel de Ville and, of course, to the newspapers.

'The discreet appearance of a brief list of press titles in the 'copies sent to' section does no harm in this type of letter. No harm at all. As you will see. You'll see the politicians jumping to it,' said Jean-Jacques.

I had my doubts but was ready to be impressed if the plan worked. Also, I couldn't help feeling a childish glow of pleasure at the thought of my signature arriving on the President's desk the following morning. True, it would be in the company of several hundred others, but, heading the list as it did, it would be the name of Peter Ferguson that caught the eye, even though – I realised –

it would hardly be the eye of Tonton himself.

*

I found an answer-phone message from Joe. Antoine was in hospital. Could I meet Joe at six in the café near République, Le Kabylie, where I had first met Antoine?

'Goddam appendicitis,' said Joe when I arrived. 'It's so banal. Why couldn't he have something romantic like consumption like any halfway decent lover?'

'Or a hernia perhaps?' I said.

Joe looked at me. 'I'm not at all sure about this new tendency of yours to make jokes. I feel it could have unpredictable effects on our relationship. Anyway, appendicitis it was. We thought of food poisoning when he woke up in the middle of the night coughing up God knows what. And since we'd both eaten the same dinner –whose ingredients I no longer wish to remember – I guessed it was only a matter of time before it got me too. But it didn't. In the end I called the *pompiers* – never call an ambulance, Peter, the fire brigade are vastly more efficient – and we were at the hospital in next to no time. Now everyone knows there's this spot you have to press to check for a burst appendix. Well, would you believe it took an hour to locate the only person on duty who could remember which spot it was? Anyway they admitted him and he was operated this morning. I stayed till he came to – that was a couple of hours ago – squeezed his hand and let him go back to sleep.'

'How was he?'

'Didn't have much of an idea what was going on. He was very concerned that his hair was uncombed. I left him my own comb on the bedside table. It'll give him something to do when he wakes in the night.'

I asked, 'How long are they keeping him in?'

'All being well, just tonight and tomorrow night. It's as straight-forward these days as pruning a rose bush. But it's when he's discharged that the problems start. I'm worried about how he'll be looked after when he first comes out.'

'Why not let him go to his parents?' I asked. 'Or to whichever one of them he gets on with.'

'His mother. That would be fine. Unfortunately his father's at home this week and he won't go there then. What a family, though. Catholic mother, Communist father, failed marriage but no divorce, no money to live separately, children taking sides et cetera, et cetera. Only good thing is, his father's a long distance truck driver and not often at home. Except this week.'

'Then maybe this is the moment for him to move in with you,' I said.

'You know,' Joe said. 'I think you may be absolutely right for once.' Then he changed the subject. 'How's the petition going? The one for whatshername – Mrs Muesli.'

'Almuslih. Too early to say. It's been sent off. Repercussions have yet to ... er ... repercuss.'

'Be careful,' Joe warned. 'Remember...'

'I know,' I said. The road to hell is paved with good Samaritans.' That was a phrase of Joe's, which he often used, and I rather liked. 'But don't worry. Nothing's going to go wrong. What could? Either it'll work – which is great – or it won't and things will stay as they were before we...'

'Started interfering?' Joe suggested.

The *patron* Momo joined us for a second. He slapped Joe on the shoulder. 'Look at him,' he said to me. 'See how happy he's become since he met his young friend. He's a new person. His eyes shine like black stars and his cheeks glow like two apples.'

'Merde,' said Joe, squirming, 'it's the sun does that, that's all.' Momo gave us a smile that could have launched a brand of toothpaste and moved off.

Looking back at me, Joe said, setting a new course without so much as a twist of his glass-stem, 'I don't see much of you these days. But your eyes are looking quite star-shiny too, if I may say so. Sure you're not having an affair of the heart yourself at long last – somewhere deep in the Marais?'

Now it was I who twisted my glass-stem, so violently that I nearly spilled the contents. 'Ha!' I said, then stopped, having no idea what I would say next. For inspiration I looked at Joe. 'Your glass is empty,' was what I came up with.

That was the beginning of a long evening with Joe. It was Friday night. Régine was back for the weekend, so I wouldn't have been spending time with Fabrice in any case. We had dinner in a restaurant Joe knew but which I didn't. We had some more drinks. We talked about pretty much everything... Except Fabrice. Then I walked home.

As I fiddled with the door-code buttons my fingers found a ragged piece of paper that had been wedged between the electric box of tricks and the wall. It had my name on it, hastily scribbled. Unfolded, it read: *Désolé que tu ne sois pas là. Il faut que nous parlions. Bisous. F.*

This was very out of character for Fabrice. Whatever he thought we needed to talk about, it was presumably something that couldn't be said over the phone or in front of Régine. Well, that last bit wasn't so very odd. Pretty well everything we said and did together these days was unfit for Régine's eyes and ears. But scrawled notes at midnight? There was nothing to do but wait, with considerable apprehension, because good news was never conveyed like this – until I had a chance to speak to Fabrice alone, which might not be till after the weekend.

NINETEEN

I went to the Figeac that Saturday evening just in case. Fabrice might well turn up, with or without Régine, and perhaps we'd be able to have the talk that Fabrice appeared to want so urgently.

Dominique was not standing at the bar of the Figeac when I arrived and neither was Fabrice or anyone else which was perhaps fortunate since – as René told me, standing in the kitchen doorway – the new waitress was late for work and his mother, who usually did not arrive till later, was not answering her phone. Not only that but some people would be arriving any minute to hang paintings in the little exhibition space downstairs. René looked to be under stress. I volunteered, for reasons that were not entirely altruistic, to serve behind the bar until the staffing situation should improve. René seemed relieved and disappeared back into the kitchen. It was then that I spotted Dominique at a table at the back of the restaurant in conclave with two other men. Clearly they wanted to be as inconspicuous as possible, since they had chosen the darkest corner of the place for their whispered conversation. On the other hand, the facts that the two strangers were dressed in full Foreign Legion uniform and that rolls of bank-notes were being furtively exchanged for small sealed packets assured them of the undivided attention of the small number of people already at the other tables. Everybody saw and everybody very deliberately didn't look. After a moment the legionnaires left and Dominique came up to the bar.

If he was surprised to see me standing behind it he chose not to show it. I poured him a pastis.

A few minutes later the waitress appeared, breathless and apologetic. The traffic had been important, she said. That the English language described such traffic as heavy would have struck her as comical. Though both pleasant and attractive, the new waitress lacked those indefinable qualities that made her predecessor Marianne so special. But her arrival did at least allow me to return to the other side of the bar.

The phone rang in the kitchen. I heard René answer it. 'Oh there you are,' he said. 'Where were you an hour ago when I needed you? Clothilde has only just got here. The clients were having to serve themselves...' There then followed a remarkably long pause before he said, in a very different tone of voice, 'Yes. Yes, I'll tell him.' René appeared in the doorway. 'Dominique. Can you go to my mother's immediately? She's got someone there she wants you to meet. Apparently it's important.'

Dominique made a grimace at me and gave a resigned shrug. 'Sorry,' he said. *'A tout à l'heure.'* Then he turned and went out of the door. Not for the first time I received a strong signal that if Madame Touret said jump, you jumped.

And then Fabrice arrived – with Régine and Jeannette and Denis. They were all planning to dine and asked me to join them at the big table. It was not the moment for private chats, though Fabrice and I found ourselves exchanging what might have been meaningful glances had there been any way of communicating what the meaning was.

The main subject of discussion was the absentee from the big table that night: Françoise. She had disappeared. Her shop was shut; 'Closed until further notice' was on the door. At her apartment the concierge understood that she had gone to Portugal on holiday, had even seen her loading bags into a taxi bound for the airport. But inspection of the apartment had shown it to be almost denuded of personal effects; far more had gone than was consistent with a Mediterranean holiday. A number of possible scenarios were constructed around these bare facts over dinner and the discussion was only brought to an end by the re-entry into the Figeac's smoky atmosphere of Dominique.

But it was a new Dominique that appeared in our midst, blazing like a meteor. For an uncharitable moment I put the change down to an excess of pastis but this misapprehension was put paid to when he sat himself down in the chair from which Françoise could not have been more conspicuously absent and announced in a voice edged with hysteria, *'J'ai un boulot, un boulot, un boulot.'* Dominique had been offered a job.

Nobody had ever imagined he wanted one.

'It's with Launier, the wine-shop chain. I'm going to be the manager of one of their outlets. After a training course, that is, and a trial period.'

Blank looks of astonishment had to be hastily reworked into congratulatory smiles. But Denis blurted out the question that everyone else was thinking. 'Isn't that a bit like putting the fox in charge of the chickens?'

Dominique smiled broadly and made a lengthy pantomime out of lighting a cigarette before replying. 'I know what you mean, but you really won't have to worry. You see, I have a secret weapon. Only for the moment it's very, very secret. But in a few days' time you'll understand everything.'

'It was an old friend of Madame Touret,' Dominique continued. 'Visiting unexpectedly. He's in Human Resources at Launier. Madane Touret thought of me and so...' It all sounded too simple. I wondered if Dominique's old tendency to fantasise was getting another airing following his rapid ingestion earlier of pastis – plus who knew what besides. Dominique singled me out for his final remark on the subject. 'As we say in France, it isn't so much what you know as who you know.'

'We say something similar in Britain,' I said.

The people who were going to arrive and hang paintings had now started to do just that, and were weaving their way between tables with framed and mounted canvasses. None of these was very big, fortunately, since not only did they all have to be manoeuvred past the seated diners but carted down the small open-work spiral staircase that led to the oak-beamed basement exhibition-room and – among other facilities – the toilets. After a while I announced that I was going downstairs to have a look at the new paintings as they were hung. I didn't ask if anyone wanted to join me. If anyone did, they would.

The canvasses were certainly bright, there was no denying that. Great splodges of brilliance overlay earlier splatterings of the same in vividly contrasting tones. It was as if the bespattered ground beneath a pigeon roost had been rendered in Technicolor. But having taken on board the aggressive dynamic of the paintings, I found myself unable to come to any critical conclusion about them. Where modern art was concerned I was an ignoramus, and if I caught the eye of one or other of the people who were doing the hanging I was shamed into turning away again with a nodding pretence of sage and thoughtful appreciation. But that didn't have to last long. The pictures had nearly all been put up by the time I came downstairs and the hangers soon all departed.

Which was the cue for Fabrice, who must have carefully counted the people down the stairs and then counted them all up again, to descend the spiral stairway himself. I watched his corkscrew progress as he materialised bit by bit: familiar trainers; unmistakeable jeans-clad legs – rangy, comfortable, strong; generously cut white shirt. Then he crossed the floor to where I stood. He took both my hands in his own as soon as he reached me.

'Careful,' I whispered.

'I'm sorry,' Fabrice said, his voice also a whisper. 'I

didn't get a chance to tell you before now. Italy's over. Régine's back for good.'

'It's not a huge surprise,' I said coolly. 'That was going to happen sometime soon anyway. We were hardly imagining a scenario in which she didn't.'

Fabrice let go of my hands. He looked a little hurt. 'You sound as though it doesn't bother you very much,' he said flatly.

'I don't mean that.' I grabbed his hands back and held them. 'It's just that I'm being realistic. I have been all along. It would have been stupid to pretend things were other than they were. It's been great. Special.' I looked up into Fabrice's eyes and saw this wasn't going down too well. 'Look, I'm sorry, I don't know what you want me to say. We'll still be … I mean, there may be other times…' I couldn't finish the thought, didn't want to hear myself say, '…when Régine isn't in the way.'

'Yeah, OK. But that's not all. I mean that's all I had to tell you when I called round last night. But now there's something else. The bank want me back in Strasbourg. This time for keeps.'

'I see,' I said. Then, *'Merde.'* I tried to tell myself that something simple and ordinary was coming to an end, some practical arrangement; that it was like having to part with a particularly helpful colleague at work who was going on to better things. Only it didn't feel like that at all.

'Yes,' said Fabrice. *'Merde.'*

'When… I mean, how soon?'

'Next month.'

'Then we've still got…' I didn't finish this either. We hadn't still got anything. In the silence Fabrice unhooked his hands from mine and placed their palms flat on my stomach, then, undoing the shirt buttons, ran them underneath the cloth and over my bare skin, exploring upward to my nipples, which were suddenly hard, then forced his fingers down behind my waistband into the familiar secret place inside my jeans.

'For Christ's sake,' I hissed at him. 'It's public. Someone'll come down. Régine…'

But the very public nature of this unanticipated intimacy excited me – an excitement that Fabrice's exploring fingers quickly discovered and then seized on, while I found my own fingers unable to resist fumbling at Fabrice's fly.

'I don't want…' Fabrice was whispering urgently at my ear. 'I can't bear to lose you now.'

'You can't have everything,' I said rather roughly, feeling that Fabrice was being even more selfish than I was. 'You've got a girlfriend.' I made the discovery at that moment that Fabrice had nothing under his jeans except himself, as ready for action, jumping up and wet-tongued, as a puppy invited for an outing.

'It's not the same. I sort of love Régine and we'll probably get married one day. But I don't have with her what I have with you.'

'You mean you can't make it with her?' I asked incredulously, hardly able to believe I was coming out with such prurient questions in this exposed place, where Régine's laughter and the conversation of her friends could be heard drifting down the open stairs ...while at the same time I was brazenly massaging her boyfriend's jutting cock.

'Not the mechanics: they're no problem. It's just the ... everything else.'

'Oh God, no.' Public place or no, the mechanics were working just fine right there and then for me. Perhaps it was for the best. It was after all the simplest way to bring this conversation to an end. I climaxed suddenly, hotly, causing Fabrice immediately to do the same, and then the sound of creaking boards alerted us both to someone coming down the stairs.

The feet and legs that first appeared were male, which was a bit of a mercy; they didn't belong to Régine. They belonged, it became apparent after one more heart-stopped second, to Denis. Fabrice and I were somehow zipped – *lightning closures* the French language aptly calls zip-fasteners, and thank God tonight for both our pairs of jeans being fitted with them, not buttons – but my white shirt still gaped incriminatingly.

Denis's mouth fell as wide open as my shirt and for a moment everyone stayed where they were, silent and rigid with surprise. Then Denis gave a sort of shrug, a nervous half smile and said, a little uncertainly, 'Well, we're all different, I suppose.' But it was what he said next that Fabrice and I would bless him for for the rest of our lives. 'Look, er ... if you guys would like to use the wash-room first, I'll hold off out here and take a look at the paintings.'

TWENTY

Joe was initiating me into the game of Pétanque in the dust bath that served as a bowling green in front of the building that housed the national archives. I thought it was about time I did something a little more active now that, with the permanent return of Régine to Fabrice's bed, my exuberant two-month burst of sexual activity had so abruptly come to an end. Something more active, at any rate, than sitting at café tables alone and brooding over glasses of beer. I'd been a passable cricketer as a schoolboy but hadn't kept it up. I'd taken up no sport in adult life except jogging.

'The beauty of Pétanque,' explained Joe, 'is that not only is it sociable and relaxing but it's easy. *En plus*, you can be as lazy as you like and no-one shouts at you.'

'Nobody shouts at you jogging either,' I said.

'Okay, but it's pretty strenuous. Dangerous too. I heard of someone who lost an eye, jogging in the Parc Monceau.'

'Lost an eye?'

'Pigeon flew up in his face. It gets very crowded there at weekends. Neither he nor it could take evasive action and its beak...'

'All right,' I said.' You've converted me.'

'Well then. With this game a novice can play with and

against the experts with no loss of enjoyment to anyone. You leave the classy shots to the old hands at first, or for ever if you want to, and go for the easy ones, like this.' He trundled a silvery ball across the uneven surface. It took a wavering path, throwing up a little cloud of white dust as it went, and finally came to rest about a foot from the *cochonnet*. Joe did not say whether its eventual position was the one he had intended for it or not. Nor did I ask. Some elderly men seated on benches in the sun nearby made non-committal grunting sounds. Now it was my throw. My ball touched the *cochonnet* with a just audible click. 'Not bad,' said Joe. 'You may go far.' His own next ball fared better than its predecessor but less well than mine. 'By the way,' he said, 'I made it up about the pigeon.'

'I'm glad,' I said.

'To go back to Launier,' said Joe, at the precise moment that I delivered my next ball, which went a metre wide, 'it's funny you should mention them.' I'd just told him the news, now three days old, of Dominique's job offer. 'Antoine and I were talking about them yesterday. We toyed with the idea of taking on one of their shop management schemes ourselves.'

That startled me a lot. 'Have you gone mad?' I said.

'No,' said Joe, taken aback. 'Why should you think that?'

'Can you see yourself, a professional man, cooped up in a tiny shop all day every day, stacking wine bottles?

And not just for a month or two, for the experience – which I've done, by the way – but for a lifetime. And with Antoine. Wouldn't that spoil just everything? The banality of it. On top of each other day and night.'

'For a guy with writerly pretensions you do have a gift for disastrous metaphor. Unless it's something in your subconscious. I do know what you mean, though. Can I say, simply, that I've thought about it and I'm not worried?'

Old men on nearby benches nodded their heads in unconscious agreement. Without understanding the words they had picked up Joe's air of conviction.

'You're very sure of the strength of your relationship, aren't you?' I said.

Joe looked at me in astonishment. 'I don't get you. One week you're delighted for the pair of us. Urging Antoine to move into my flat. The next you're full of doubts about us. What's changed for you?' He looked at me narrowly. 'Something gone wrong in your own love life? The one I know nothing about?'

I couldn't say anything. I'd have cried if I'd tried to speak. I was conscious of Joe staring at me, peering deep into the emptiness of my silence. Then he said gently, 'Sorry if I've scored a bulls-eye. Didn't mean to pry.'

'I can't talk about it,' I said.

I threw my next ball idly in the air. By chance it landed, bomb-like, in the centre of the cluster of balls that vied for proximity to the *cochonnet*, scattering them in all directions. It took up its own station a snug half centimetre from the *cochonnet* itself and a metre from the nearest competition. 'Bravo!' shouted the old men. One even got to his feet and clapped.

'Je-sus!' said Joe. 'I never saw a beginner do that.'

At that moment a figure hailed us from the other side of the street. It was Antoine.

'What the hell are you doing here?' Joe asked him when he had crossed over to us, making a brave attempt to disguise the fact that he still walked with a slight limp. 'You're supposed to be still convalescing back at the apartment.'

'As it happens,' said Antoine airily, 'I've felt quite strong since lunchtime. I've spent the afternoon sunbathing in the park.'

'Hope you didn't run into any pigeons,' I said.

I suggested that the three of us dine at the the Figeac. The others took that up. There was the removal of Antoine's stitches to be celebrated. The operation had been performed that morning.

'But be careful you don't eat too much,' Joe told him. 'You might burst.'

'Arrête!' protested Antoine with an involuntary shudder. 'You make my legs go all funny!'

As we arrived at the restaurant a television crew were

loading their equipment into a van in the street outside. We went in and found Jean-Jacques at the bar, improbably dressed, despite the broiling weather, in a three-piece woollen suit and a bow tie. 'What have we missed?' I asked.

'Things are beginning to happen,' said Jean-Jacques. 'Just beginning. They've filmed the shop, the interior as well as outside, and they interviewed Madame Almuslih. It went off very well. She was clear and articulate and sobbed at exactly the right moment when she spoke of her children. An actress could not have gauged it better. After that they interviewed Madame Touret and...' Modesty obliged him to hesitate.

'And you of course,' Joe put in helpfully. 'When will they show it?'

'Tomorrow at seven on the regional bulletin, just after the *météo*, all being well. If there's a riot or a plane crash they'll show it the day after.'

'Excellent,' I said.

'That's not all. *Le Monde* and *Libération* had reporters here this morning and *Le Parisien* arrived after lunch with a photographer. *Le Figaro* may come tomorrow.'

'Congratulations,' said Joe. 'You obviously knew what you were doing.'

'Would someone please explain what this is all about?' Antoine asked, not unreasonably since this was his first visit to the Figeac and he had expected a steak, not a press conference. In addition, he had been the centre of everyone's attention for the past six days and it was rather a shock to his convalescent system to be reminded that this state would not last for ever.

We put Antoine in the picture as we made our way to the big table. No-one else sat there yet. Joe asked casually, 'Your friend Fabrice likely to join us?'

Although it shouldn't have done, that gave me a jolt. I answered too quickly, without thought. 'No. Actually Régine's back now.'

Joe stared at me. I saw in his eyes a chain of connections being forged among his thoughts. He hadn't guessed about Fabrice and me before that moment. But now, I could see, he had.

Just then a most unlikely thing happened. Jean-Jacques asked if he might join us. I'm ashamed to say I felt relief at that. Joe might or might not have been tempted to pursue enquiries about Fabrice and me in front of Antoine, but he wasn't going to do so in the company of Jean-Jacques.

But also I was astonished at Jean-Jacques' request. I'd never seen so much as a crumb pass his lips before now, but as the convivial meal got under way I watched a plate of charcuterie disappear between the poet's bearded jaws, followed by a *magret de canard au poivre*, with the kind of fascination I usually reserved for watching a fire eater or sword swallower. I wondered if I'd ever feel quite the same about French poetry again.

Joe asked him casually where Dominique was.

'He'll be in later, I expect,' said Jean-Jacques, 'with Marianne.'

In the firmament of Paris's eternal feminine Marianne shone brightly where I was concerned. I missed her presence at the Figeac all the more in the aftermath of my severance from Fabrice and it had occurred to me that it would not be impossible to track her down. It was time I returned to more mainstream pursuits after my uncharacteristic – I didn't even think the word *homosexual* – dalliance with a male friend. I thought perhaps a new relationship, of whatever sort, with a woman might do my self-image some good. It might not have been appropriate to ask Dominique about Marianne but I'd thought I might try Madame Touret. I just hadn't got round to it yet.

Now it was a shock to hear she'd be arriving any minute in the company of Dominique, Only Antoine, who was sitting directly opposite me, picked up on my discomfiture. 'Who is Marianne?' he asked Jean-Jacques.

'Dominique's fiancée,' he said. 'They got engaged two days ago.' He turned to me. 'Did you not know that?'

Paris. Mid-summer. 1987

I walked down to the quai du Louvre. It was night. The lamps glittered through the trees and their gold reflections quavered in the dark water of the Seine as it rippled past. I stopped at the place I'd stopped at last time and lit a cigarette. Nobody came out from the shadows under the trees. After a while I dived deep into the shadows myself. When my eyes got used to the darkness I found I was almost on top of two men who were standing facing each other, their trousers down to their knees, each pulling on the other's jutting cock.

I started to back away, concerned for their privacy, but apparently I didn't need to do that. One of the guys turned his head towards me and with his free hand beckoned me to join them. I moved towards them, unzipping, springing my trapped hard cock, and pulling my jeans down a little way as I took the three or four steps that brought me within their arms' reach. We formed a sort of triangle with our forearms, each one of us jerking another one's cock. We carried on masturbating together, the three of us, for about a minute.

Then one of the guys gasped urgently, 'Je jouis,' and proceeded to erupt immediately, covering my hand with his hot milk. I went on tugging him until he had completely finished. He let me know when that point was reached by saying, 'OK. Ça suffit.'

The other one then said to me, 'You want to fuck?'

'Me you, or you me?' I said.

He said, 'You do me.' He reached down awkwardly into a pocket, currently at knee height. He handed me a condom. 'Put that on,' he said. I did.

He took a couple of hobbling paces away from me.

Just far enough to prop himself against the nearest chestnut trunk. I hobbled after him, and so did the other guy – the one who'd just shot his bolt. He hadn't pulled his jeans back up either.

The guy who'd invited me to fuck him now had his chest against the tree-trunk. I prised apart the cheeks of his arse with my hands. Fabrice and I had never done it standing up. This guy was taller than I was. I could only get inside him with the tip of my dick. I had to ask him to bend his knees a bit. He did that, and then I got all the way inside him and started to fuck. Meanwhile the third guy got his hand between my guy and the tree trunk and went back to work on his cock.

I came after a matter of seconds. The novelty of the situation had got the better of me. I pulled out, and he, the guy I'd just been inside, twisted back around so I could see him coming when the third guy's hand brought him to his climax a few seconds after that. Then I pulled my jeans up over my still hard and condom-clad dick. The jeans would have to go in the wash.

I touched the other two lightly on the shoulders, one hand each. All three of us said a quiet, 'Bonne nuit.' Then I left them. Their trousers were still down. I had the impression they were considering another wank.

Walking along the path beside the river I found a litter bin. I got right up to it and pulled my now flaccid cock out, right over the bin. I pulled the condom off and dropped it into it.

The Paris Novel

*

That night the cushion of hot air that had been threatening to smother Paris for days was ripped open by shears of lightning and its substance scattered on the wind. Night had succeeded sweltering night and by now all Paris was sleeping with its windows wide open if it slept at all. It was nearly three in the morning when the wind got up that set all those windows banging, chimneys shrieking, and flower pots crashing from balconies. The opera-set sprang into life as dressing-gowned figures appeared, back-lit, all across the city, fastening shutters and reining in geraniums. Ten minutes later the sky was on fire with lightning and the air cannoning with thunder. When at last the rain fell it seemed as though an airborne ocean had been shot down over Paris. Its last remnants were still draining down when I went out in the morning. Grey clouds still blew across the drenched city like smoke over the scene of a finished battle. The Métro was out of action due to flooding and the buses were impossibly full, and le tout Paris went to work on foot.

Anthony McDonald

TWENTY-ONE

The official celebration of Dominique's engagement to Marianne took place the following week. Dominique had invited all Paris with the exception, he said, of the Parisians. By that time the city had recovered from its soaking: water-filled awnings over shops had been emptied out by prodding with brooms, café tables had dried off in the returning sunshine and my thermometer was climbing past thirty once again in the late afternoons. Madame Almuslih's photograph had appeared in the papers and, because there had been neither riot nor plane crash, an audience of millions had witnessed her tears in between a promise of continuing fine weather and a report on the plague of aphids which were munching their way through the exotics in the gardens of Versailles.

The Figeac was transformed for the evening. Most of the chairs had been removed and stacked in the exhibition room at the foot of the spiral stairs. The tables were reincarnated, thanks to immaculate white cloths as big as sails, as a seamless buffet that lined the walls. I'd lived in France just long enough not to be surprised by the scale and variety of the refreshments but I was impressed all the same. There were salads of artichoke hearts and endive, lettuce and walnut, tomatoes and fresh basil that scented the room. In small bowls were quails' eggs to be eaten with the fingers, and sticks of carrot and celery to be dipped in garlic mayonnaise. There were cold poached salmon trout and boiled langoustines that rattled when you picked them up. For the moment that was all. Hot roasts of meat and poultry would materialise later when there was room. Room on the tables, I wondered, or room in the guests? There was champagne – rows of bottles in a trough of iced water – and crates of red wine from Cahors, courtesy of Madame Touret's family connections in the region.

'Who in the world is paying for it all?' I asked Jean-Jacques. 'Surely even the cannabis connection doesn't provide Dominique with the means for all this?'

'Madame Touret pays. At least, the business does.'

'But why? It's not as if he was family, after all.' Even as I said this I guessed that I was being stupidly naïf. I was still a foreigner and a newcomer after all. No doubt a dozen veils of nuance still came between me and any real contact with French life.

Jean-Jacques looked pained, like an adult who has to spell out for a child something that usually does not have to be mentioned. 'Strictly speaking that's true. Both Dominique's parents are dead. His surname is the same as his mother's, if you get me, but his father was Madame Touret's brother. His own widow and their children will have nothing to do with Dominique, and Madame Touret is, by default, his nearest living blood relation. Now, if I may say this to you, Peter, this is one of those things that everybody knows without having to remember all the time. Do you understand?'

'Of course. That explains...' It explained so much that

I decided at once not to bore Jean-Jacques by listing it all. 'But such a lavish buffet...' I headed off hurriedly on a different tack. 'How will they cap this at the wedding?'

'That's the French way. The wedding is for Marianne's parents to lose sleep over, not for Madame Touret and certainly not for us. Madame Touret can breathe a big sigh of relief after tonight. Her opinion is that Dominique will be as safe in harness with Marianne as he could be with anyone. In other words, she's very pleased at the results of her efforts.'

This shed even more light on the power and influence of Madame Touret. She had probably even employed Marianne in the first instance with the present moment in mind. I was doubly glad I hadn't asked her for news of Marianne a week ago.

'Now, *à propos*, let me show you this.' Jean-Jacques fished a letter from his pocket. It was from the Ministry of Justice and not *à propos* at all. It concerned the Almuslihs. I read it, picking my way through the florid formulae with some difficulty, but I discerned at last a promise to re-examine the husband's dossier and to investigate all possible ways to limit the financial liability of the wife. 'So far, so good,' said Jean-Jacques. 'A little force exerted by the media can work wonders with the people who control our lives. The press is not so called for nothing. Now the room is filling up. You'd better go and get something to eat and drink before it all goes.' The name of the letter's signatory had struck me as familiar. F. Guyot. Guyot ... of course: Margueritte d'Alabouvettes' son in law, the man from the ministry.

Of the people I hadn't yet met, I was able to guess which ones were guests of Dominique's and which were Marianne's by their different dress styles: Marianne's tending to a bourgeois smartness, Dominique's displaying a more raffish brand of chic. Among those I did know, sartorial style was equally varied. Joe had come in jeans and trainers, Antoine in a suit. Fabrice and Régine seemed dressed for a society wedding while Denis and Jeannette appeared to have dressed down for the occasion on purpose. I found himself wishing for Françoise, simply to see what her dress sense would have made of the evening.

In her absence there was at least some news of her; it arrived via Jeannette. '*Grandes tractations*,' she said. 'A big carry-on. Half the stock has gone from the shop, and none of it paid for. Her suppliers are doing their pieces. So's her landlord. She was four months behind with the rent, it seems.'

'And any news from herself?' I asked.

'A postcard from Portugal. No address, of course. She says she knows she's done the right thing and intends to stay there for ever. She sounds as though she's gone crazy.'

'I see,' I said. Actually I saw a beautifully sane logic at the root of the whole thing. Françoise had wanted the sunshine first and foremost and then a man as a means to that end. She had quite deliberately pursued the wish and now she had it. The fact that the man in the case was now in prison was quite possibly not a disadvantage at all. No, I could not consider Françoise crazy.

Madame Touret asked me if I felt at home yet in the *quartier*. 'We all feel you are part of the place now,' she said, and the conventional formula touched me somehow: reassuring me after my recent discovery that I'd failed to pick up on the relationship between her and Dominique. But it was a small consolation prize for the unexpected feeling of emptiness I was experiencing following my banishment from Fabrice's bed.

'Thank you,' I said. I tried to feel positive. It was true that I'd found a social circle in which I felt comfortable. I'd made a number of friends. I'd made progress with the language to the extent that I could express everything I wanted to say clearly if not always beautifully. No-one would yet take me for a Frenchman once I opened my mouth, but then no-one ever would. I was still unsure whether the word for street-lamp was masculine or feminine but as time passed it seemed to matter less and less. I mentioned this to Madame Touret.

'Réverbère est masculin,' she said, in a tone as puzzled as if she'd been asked whether water was dry or wet.

The buffet tables were now reloaded, this time with baskets of potatoes, jacket-baked and wrapped in foil, fragrant garlic bread, leafy salads and roast joints of beef, ducks and guinea fowl. Marianne arrived with two glasses of red wine. 'Can you tell the difference?' she asked. 'One's Bergerac, the other's Cahors.'

I sniffed at both, took a sip from one, made a few faces such as I'd seen professional tasters do, and swallowed. 'Cahors,' I pronounced. 'Cahors always tastes of damsons.' I repeated the process with the second glass. 'Oh,' I said, a bit deflated. 'They both taste of damsons.'

'Cheer up,' Marianne said. 'They're both Cahors. You're the only person so far who's realised. I'm getting in practice for the training course. It starts in September. Then there's a six-month trial period in a Launier branch in boulevard Haussman. After that, well, it could be anywhere in Paris, depending on which *quartier* vacancies arise in.' She moved off to undermine the wine-tasting confidence of someone else.

Antoine appeared at my elbow. I offered him the two glasses of red wine to try. 'Which one's the Cahors?'

He gulped at both glasses of wine without ceremony and swallowed. 'They're both Cahors,' he said simply.

Joe arrived. 'There's going to be a strike tomorrow,' he said.

'Who says?' I asked.

Joe raised his eyebrows a bit camply. 'Your friend Fabrice told me. It's gonna be the Métro, the buses and the suburban trains. The whole works.'

'It's nothing to worry about,' said Antoine. 'They're always doing it. It never amounts to more than a *grève de zèle*.'

'What's that?' I asked.

Joe answered. 'A partial strike. A go slow, if you like. But Antoine's wrong. This time it looks like they're going to go the whole hog.' Now it was Antoine's turn to ask for a translation.

Jean-Jacques brushed past us. 'I'm going to look for a kir. This champagne is playing havoc with my liver,' we heard him mutter as he passed.

'Why is his liver so different from everyone else's,' Antoine wondered out loud when the poet was out of earshot, 'that a few glasses of champagne affect it but an ocean of kir does not?'

'Because,' I said, 'he sold his liver to the devil in return for his talent and now it operates differently as a result.' I was delighted at having just for once left Antoine lost for a reply.

Fabrice came up and caught me by the arm. We'd exchanged little more than a couple of sentences all evening. 'Come on,' he said. 'Let's go and see the paintings downstairs.'

'We saw them last week,' I said.

He smiled and his eyes twinkled. He said in English, 'Don't be a dick.'

We trod down the spiral stairs, Fabrice first, me following. At the bottom Fabrice turned to me and said, 'Antoine's cute.'

I said, 'You're going to have to make your mind up one of these days, you know.'

For a moment Fabrice looked older than his thirty years. He said, 'That's a luxury I just don't have. Whereas you...'

'How do you mean, *whereas me*?' I said.

'You're freer than a bird, Peter. You don't have anyone else's expectations to consider. But being gay or otherwise is not a lifestyle choice that I can make.'

I leant back against the wall, my shoulder nudging one furiously scarlet painting just a bit askew. I said, 'Look, I just don't get this. I get Joe telling me endlessly that being gay is not a lifestyle choice: you either are or aren't, or so he says. Now here you come and tell me the exact opposite. I wish you'd all make up your bloody minds.'

'It isn't a contradiction,' Fabrice said. He was struggling with his thoughts a bit. He'd had quite a lot to drink. 'Joe's talking about who you are, I think, and I'm on about what you're actually allowed to do. Whatever I am – whatever that is – and I'm less sure about what that is now that I've met you than I was before (because, by the way, knowing you has made me question everything about myself, but we'll leave that for the moment) – where was I? – lifestyle, yeah. You see, I can only go one way. I come from a *bonne famille*, you see, and Régine from another. You hate all that idea, I know you do, and I do care what you think, Peter...' He reached out a hand and tentatively touched my shirt-front. 'I care more about you than I've ever had the guts to let you see.' He shrugged. 'Born with a silver spoon, if you like, so that makes me lucky. But still, that's what's expected of me in that situation: marry Régine and be a family man; carry on the line; that's how it goes.'

Fabrice looked so unhappy, almost distraught, during this speech, that I felt really sorry for him, almost experienced his pain. Yet in a way I felt gratified too. I'd clearly made a difference to Fabrice. I was partly the cause of the feelings that were tearing him apart. I might be just about to disappear into Fabrice's past, but I was evidently not going to go unremembered, without leaving a mark. Fabrice had been close to saying something just now, I realised, that would have shaken still further the foundations of both our worlds. I was glad it hadn't come to that. I didn't think I could have coped if Fabrice's ramblings had reached their probable destination of – in either French or English – *I love you.*

'Or else you have to lead a double life,' I heard myself say. I wasn't sure if I meant that Fabrice already did lead a double life, or that I was now leading a double life myself. I decided to put my uncertainty down to the fact that I too was getting slightly drunk.

'I think I mustn't do that,' I heard Fabrice say. 'I think I've got to try and give all I've got, all that I am, to Régine. To try at any rate. Hope for the best.'

This is good-bye, then, I thought; this is that moment, suddenly now. And that was the moment when the domino tower inside me – the domino tower that was me – finally collapsed. I wanted to cry. I wanted Fabrice to take me in his arms and hold me, protect me from the world and from myself, for ever.

'We move out of Paris at the end of next week,' Fabrice said flatly. 'There'll be a few drinks in here before we go.' He brushed at my close-cropped beard with the back of his fingers. I stood still for a moment and let myself be caressed, then I leaned in slowly towards Fabrice and kissed him on the lips, then, in my own time leaned back out again. That kiss marked the end of our affair.

We made an intensely silent circuit of the exhibition that was mounted on the walls around us. It occurred to me that there was a connection between the violent brightness of the canvasses that seemed so articulate of something un-guessable and hidden, and the turmoil that was going on inside the pair of us viewing them. A turmoil that could not be articulated in any other way.

The party lasted till the early hours even if the champagne did not. When the food was finished, guitars and an accordion were produced from nowhere and there was dancing, though only a little as the space was too small to take more than a couple of couples at a time. I danced once, a little unsteadily, with Madame Touret and once with Marianne and considered that I'd done my duty. At one point Joe and Antoine danced together quite unselfconsciously and without apparently shocking anyone. Fabrice made a move to invite me to follow suit with him, but I shook my head. Even though Denis had discovered our secret and Joe had deduced it I had no intention of announcing it so brazenly to Régine and everybody else. Especially as the affair was now ended.

Dominique made a speech which no-one, least of all he, would remember in the morning and then it was suddenly time to go. Numbers thinned quickly and soon I found myself, one of the last to leave, outside in the cool air of early morning.

I headed down to the river bank.

TWENTY-TWO

For the second time in ten days most of Paris had to walk to work. The first time it had been because the Métro was flooded following the storm, this second time it was the strike. I didn't have to join the marching hordes. I was a writer. My mission was, as Hemingway so memorably put it, to stay home and write.

But I wanted – needed – to be out and about. Fabrice would be gone from my life in a few more days. I was having difficulty coping with that idea. I thought it might be marginally easier to deal with it in the wide open boulevards of the city than in the confines of my small apartment.

Following the quays from the Hôtel de Ville to the Pont des Arts I crossed the river towards the elegant façade of the Institut de France. Later in the day the bridge would be hung with pictures and jammed with the people who painted, bought and sold them. But at this hour there was nothing to be seen save the original views.

To the left the Ile de la Cité lay in midstream like a giant battleship at anchor, its superstructure the brick frontages of the place Dauphine and its big guns the spires of the Conciergerie, of the Sainte Chapelle and of Notre Dame. The image was only marginally unsettled by the soft green willows that sprouted from its sharp bows. To the right the river ran past the Louvre's austere façade where pillar and window repeated like recurring decimals until halted by the elevation of the Grand Palais. Then there were the chestnut trees, a sunny froth of green along the river bank by day. In whose shadowy caverns I had casual sex with men at night.

I headed away from the river, going south. Along the straight rue de Seine and its continuation, the rue de Tournon. At last I came to the Luxembourg Garden. And in there, beneath the trees, I did what Hemingway instructed. Stayed and wrote. Trying to make the activity, the busy-ness of work, along with the summer sunshine, heal the hurt in my heart. It didn't, of course.

In the evening I walked back. I was not sorry to be stopped a little way short of my destination by an arm waving from the terrace of the Little Horseshoe. Not long ago the arm would have belonged automatically to Fabrice, but those days were past. This evening it belonged, unexpectedly, to Jean-Jacques. I'd never seen it waved before. But until the previous week I hadn't seen Jean-Jacques eat a meal or wear a suit either. Clearly his involvement with the Almuslih petition was having its effects; and when I joined the poet at his table I learnt of yet another.

He leaned across towards me. 'My old publisher was planning a reissue of some of the writings inspired by the protests of sixty-eight. It'll be the twentieth anniversary next year. He hadn't thought of me in that connection. But then he saw me on the television the other night.' Jean-Jacques paused and his face seemed almost to crack into a smile. 'This morning I had a phone-call. Have a beer.'

The streets were thick with cars making their slow way out to the périphérique and the suburbs beyond. Not everyone lived within walking distance of their work. By seven o'clock the Marais, and presumably the whole of Paris too, was gridlocked. The sounding of horns rose to a fortissimo bombardment but then died away again as one after another the drivers left their cars. All had the same idea: to telephone their wives, husbands, relatives or friends to say they would be late – and to do it now. Mobiles were still a rarity and an unrealistic queue formed in the doorway of the Horseshoe for the café's single payphone.

Jean-Jacques beckoned to the barman. 'Why don't you take drinks orders from the phone queue? You have a captive clientèle, all irritable and thirsty. There's money to be made, don't you think? I give you this suggestion for nothing.' The idea was taken up, developed, borrowed by the other cafés in the street and by seven-thirty the street was busy with pencil-thin, penguin-dressed waiters and their aproned bosses with their different figures, less pencil than brandy glass. They were zigzagging among the stationary traffic as if the cars were so many closely packed tables. Trays of glasses were balanced on their upturned palms as they uncapped bottles, took money, poured glasses of cool white wine, dispensed mint tea, shandies and mineral waters. A traffic jam was transformed into a street party.

'C'est pas pour rien qu'on dit un bouchon,' said Jean-Jacques. It's not called a bottle-neck for nothing.

Not until eight fifteen was the traffic on the move again. Drivers returned their empties to the cafés or at least to the nearest piece of pavement before driving away – a little regretfully, I thought. 'Not Parisians,' said Jean-Jacques. *'Banlieusards.'* The word, and especially the scornful way in which he said it made the suburbanites sound positively reptilian. 'Parisians would never return their glasses like that.'

'By the way, congratulations,' I said.

'What?'

I reminded him. 'Your poetry reissue.'

'Thank you,' he said. 'You know, I was just thinking it might be time to put together a new volume.'

'Strike while the iron's hot, you mean?'

'Such is the nature,' Jean-Jacques interrupted himself to take a small mouthful of kir, 'of what we poets call the market.'

On the news, a little later, it was announced that, the strike having been a pronounced success, no repetition was planned for the morrow.

*

I did see Fabrice again over the next few days. Sometimes at the Figeac. Always with Régine. We didn't have a proper chance to speak. We confined ourselves to pleasantries about the weather. Having to do that hurt. Yet had we had a chance to be alone together, what would we have said? Fabrice had already laid it out on the table for me. He had to do what his family and Régine's required of him. In a way I had to respect him for that. It was no consolation to me, though, that he looked as distressed and unhappy as I felt.

Fabrice and I had been friends who'd enjoyed a bit of a fling together. We'd had sex. That had surprised me. It still did. I still identified myself as straight. Another issue was that I hadn't thought of myself as emotionally involved with Fabrice. I'd been a bit slow on the uptake there, though. Now I was about to lose him I found to my astonishment that I was hurting more horribly than I'd ever hurt before. More painfully than I'd even guessed I could be hurt. I had trouble understanding how this had come about.

Fabrice and Régine's leaving do was a bit low-key. Well, it could hardly have competed with the engagement party of Marianne and Dominique. Those two were there of course. And Jean-Jacques. Jeannette and Denis. Joe and Antoine. Myself. There were drinks at the Little Horseshoe, followed by a steak dinner at the Figeac. At one point during the evening Joe looked at me very directly and said, 'Are you all right?' I nodded my head and said brightly that I was. Then Joe gave me that look that people give you when they know you've just lied to them but are not going to be unkind enough to call your bluff.

We parted with kisses at the end of the evening. All of us. I kissed Fabrice on both cheeks. And felt I was being Judas to myself.

I also kissed Joe and Antoine goodnight. A few minutes later that was. Outside the street door of my apartment block. It lay on their route back to theirs. 'If ever you want to talk, you know...' Joe said. 'I mean, about anything at all... Well, you know I'm here for you.'

I said, 'Thank you for that.' Then I tapped out the entry code and went inside for the night.

The yellow window opposite cast its light into the sky with its usual abandon. Whoever lived there had the casements open wide but the occupant remained invisible. Not for the first time I was tempted to call across the street to see who would actually appear but of course I did not. Shyness and a fear of being ridiculous got the better of curiosity.

But this situation quickly altered once I was asleep, when dreaming seized the reins from consciousness. For then the inhabitant of the room did appear at the window, though only in silhouette. It was impossible to scrutinise the face or even guess to which sex the head belonged. I knew only that I wished to be in that room rather than in my own, and soon I found myself climbing a broad, carpeted staircase, hauling at polished mahogany banisters, flight after flight.

The staircase narrowed, was un-carpeted and dusty; it gave way to a vertical ladder clamped to a bare brick wall. At last, though I didn't know how I got there, I stood outside the door which would lead into the lighted room. I opened the door.

But dreams notoriously fail to deliver the expected goods. The room was full of ice. Full from floor to ceiling, from door to window, from wall to wall. Of any occupant whatsoever there was no sign.

I was woken by the coldness of the tears that drained across my cheeks.

Anthony McDonald

TWENTY-THREE

Paris. July. 1987.

I masturbate fiercely now that Fabrice has gone. It's as though I've regressed to being a teenager again. I'm sure it's some psychological coping mechanism that all the experts know about. But it's taken me by surprise. I do it in bed before I go to sleep at night. I do it in the morning before I get up. I do it if I wake up in the middle of the night. I do it even if I've been down earlier to the river bank.

Three weeks have passed since Fabrice went away. The pain hasn't dulled or faded in the slightest. It's like a winter split that never heals. Though it doesn't just affect a thumb or finger. My whole life has split.

As if to remind me of that, I still have difficulty getting my socks on in the morning. I manage eventually, always, but as I struggle with my numb toes I long, just as I do when masturbating, for Fabrice's tender help.

With any luck the feeling in my toes will come back eventually. Perhaps in a year, perhaps in only a few more months. And with winter splits you always have the knowledge that May will come eventually and mend your skin. But the other thing is not amenable to the healing power of time, I think. I walk around Paris in the height of summer. Bright flowers fill the parks and gardens with colour and wafts of scent. Roses, lupins, summer jasmine mingle their fragrance with the omnipresent aroma of baking baguettes.

But you know what? I have a micro-climate deep inside me and I take it with me wherever I go. To the shops. To the restaurants. To dinner at Joe and Antoine's. Perpetual winter has descended on my heart. I am the garden in the Oscar Wilde story. The story called The Selfish Giant. Summer came and went all around outside his garden, but inside his garden the winter never went. I am that garden. I am that selfish giant. With my permanently frostbitten toes.

Last night I went to the river bank again. I go there often enough now to find myself seeing – and more than merely seeing – the same people again from time to time. Last night it was the Thai fellow I'd met my first time down there. That time we'd had the pleasure of each other's cock. Last night I fucked him, standing him against the wall there with his trousers at half-mast. I was gentle with him. Although I'm not big he is the smaller of the two of us. In the end he was fine. In the end...

In the end, as I was reaching the climax, a strange thing happened. I felt that he had transformed himself somehow – or that I'd magically changed him – into the physicality of Fabrice. They are quite unalike in reality, if only in the most obvious matter of size. Fabrice is quite a big guy, and this chap is not. Yet so strong was the sensation that I found I'd whispered his name as I was coming. That made the guy snigger a moment later. He asked me, 'Who is Fabrice?'

Anthony McDonald

I said, 'Sorry about that. Fabrice is someone you're unlikely ever to meet.'

*

A few days after I wrote that I came back from shopping to find there was a message on my answerphone. There was also a letter on the mat. I dealt with the phone first. I didn't recognize the female voice for a second, but then she gave her name. It was Régine, She'd never phoned me before. She was saying there was news I needed to know, and suggesting I call back. My heart did something dizzy-making. I thought this could only be bad news about Fabrice. But also, this was a contact that took me close to Fabrice. Perhaps when I phoned back he would answer...

I so much wanted that.

I dialled the number. But it was Régine again who spoke.

'Fabrice has had to go away. He asked me to phone you.'

'Why? What's the matter? Is Fabrice OK?'

'He's fine. Don't worry. *Par contre* you may have a small problem. With Monsieur Guyot.'

'Who?' This was so remote from anything I might have been expecting that for a second I couldn't remember who that was.

'Monsieur Guyot. Son-in-law to la belle Margueritte. Apparently, when your petition landed on his desk he went ballistic.'

'What? My petition? I'm not with you.'

'You pay cash, don't you? To la belle Margueritte? Which makes you not strictly legal. You remember that Monsieur Guyot is looking for every opportunity to drop the d'Alabouvettes in the *merde*? Right. Do you remember too, that he worked for the ministère d'Urbanisme et de Logement?'

Light began to dawn.

'Yours was the first name – plus address, which happens to be the same as his ex-wife's – on that petition we all signed for the shop lady, Madame Al....er ...'

'Almuslih.'

'It's just really bad luck that it had to land on his desk out of all the others. But unfortunately you've handed him a pistol and the bullets to go with it.'

'What can I do?' I felt suddenly alarmed, suddenly isolated. Perhaps it was the word pistol that did it.

'Fabrice thinks you should get onto Margueritte as soon as possible. Put your heads together and you'll be able to sort something out, I know. But you must get on to it quickly, Fabrice says. She's very volatile. Faced with Monsieur Guyot she'll panic if left to her own devices and you'll be the one to lose out. If you want to talk to Fabrice he'll be back tomorrow.'

'Merde,' I said under my breath. But I thanked Régine for the warning, and said that I'd ring Fabrice the next day, before putting the phone down. I looked round the room. It suddenly looked less like home. I picked up the letter that was on the mat.

Its Chicago postmark would have puzzled me but for my just ended phone conversation with Régine. I tore the envelope open. In the letter, which was written by hand, Madame d'Alabouvettes informed me regretfully that her third daughter would be returning from Chile, her marriage having recently taken a nosedive – not that she put it like that – and that she would need my apartment. She would therefore be obliged to terminate my tenancy at the end of the month.

Régine's warning had come too late. No amount of negotiation would be able to dis-invent the broken marriage story. I dropped the letter into the bin and walked out of the flat.

I would have gone to talk to Joe. But he and Antoine were away. They'd gone to a wedding in Normandy. Weeks ago Joe had offered me a chance to open up to him. I'd turned the offer down. Now I wanted nothing so much as to talk to him: to say something that, whatever words I might use, would be understood by both of us to mean, *Help me.* I cursed the bride and groom whose choice of wedding date had taken my friend away to an unknown address in Normandy on this particular day.

The Paris Novel

But more than I wanted Joe, I wanted Fabrice. The image, and the sensation, came to me then of those big warm arms comfortingly around me. I longed for Fabrice. But he was out of reach, even by telephone, until tomorrow. And tomorrow never comes.

I couldn't face anyone else. Not the Kabylie café. Not the Little Horseshoe. Not the Figeac. I spent the day wandering aimlessly in the city streets.

I found myself, almost involuntarily, seeking again the mysterious bar I'd visited with Fabrice my first evening in Paris and that I hadn't rediscovered since. But it remained elusive, refusing, despite increasingly diligent searching, to show itself in the dark labyrinth of streets. I began to wonder if it had ever actually existed or if it had been simply the setting of a dream. Already the image of it was amalgamating in my mind with Van Gogh's painting of the *Café de Nuit*: the men trying to construct a battleship out of dominoes were already superimposed on the crashed-out figures slumped over Van Gogh's tables; the snake and tomato colour scheme now seemed to be common to both the insubstantial memory and the tangible painting, while the light-bulbs of the one fused with the baleful gas mantles of the other to produce a sinister hybrid light that burned into my brain. And yet it was only five months ago that the vulturine man had pulled a domino from the swaying tower and, placing it on the top, announced the hope of the world. I combed those back streets a little longer. Then I gave up my search.

The trees in the boulevards were silent so it must have

been an imaginary cold wind that I felt blowing as I strove to make some sense of what I felt. I walked without thinking about a destination through streets that appeared fuller than usual of the city's dross: the *clochards*, tramps and winos who seemed to have been washed up like flotsam on prosperity's tide, stranded in doorways and on benches among a litter of broken bottles and empty hopes. From time to time as I walked, the Eiffel Tower peered at me over the shoulders of the crowding buildings, a vulgar fairground incarnation of itself, brassy and intrusive among my painful thoughts.

I didn't go to the river bank that night, though I must have walked just about everywhere else in the city. From boulevard Magenta to the place de Clichy. From the rue de Rennes to the Gare de Montparnasse. Back across the river. Tumbling exhausted into bed.

I dreamt I was having to re-take a school exam in maths.

*

I left it as long as possible before phoning Fabrice next day. Régine had said he would be back that day. That meant travelling back from somewhere. From where, though? I hadn't asked. But he was unlikely to have returned by crack of dawn, however short the journey. He might not be back till early evening. Or later than that...

How long is it possible to put off a phone call that you desperately want, yet don't want, to make? I lasted out till two in the afternoon. I phoned then. But nobody answered, and they didn't seem to have an answerphone. That or it was on the blink. I tried again at five, and then I tried at eight. No Régine. No Fabrice.

I phoned Joe's number. It seemed they weren't back from Normandy yet, or else had gone out. At least I managed to leave a message for Joe. I said simply that when he had a spare moment there were things I wanted to talk about. Even if I wasn't sure what those things were yet.

There was some pizza in the fridge. I heated that up and had a glass of wine with it. I was still exhausted from all my walking and thinking the day before. I went early to bed.

A hammering sound came out of the depths of my slumber like something rising to the surface of a lake. It woke me at last and I lay in bed for a second or two, trying to make sense of it.

It was my door that was being banged on. It had happened before in the middle of the night. This was Dominique again. It had to be. No-one else would do this. My heart, barely wakened, sank. Had he come to tell me a second time that he'd killed Marianne? Had he – God forbid – actually done it this time. I found myself drained of any resources that I might call upon in order to help him. No energy, no ideas, no hopes.

But I did what I had to. I got out of bed, pulled a dressing-gown over my nakedness, and moved towards the door. 'Who is it?' I asked in French.

'It's me,' came from the other side. It was Fabrice.

*

He took me in his arms and I took him in mine. I broke down and wept uncontrollably, drenching the shoulder of his denim jacket with my tears, waking the night-time quietness with my rending sobs.

He pawed the back of my neck and shoulders with a desperate rough urgency. His own tears came thick and fast. He kissed me, thrusting his tongue into me for a second, then he withdrew it. In English he said, 'I love you, kid.'

The Paris Novel

TWENTY-FOUR

I will never forget our love-making that night. The way he slipped my dressing-gown off me, so that I stood there with my smaller naked body pressed up against his bigger one, still fully clothed. My hard and much-used penis lay rigid against his jeans. Those didn't stay closed to me for long though: I'd soon undone the studs of his fly; released the wagging friend that lived inside.

I undressed him completely. He led me back to my small bed. He laid me on it carefully, like a little girl arranging a doll on its back... For weeks now I'd been the guy in charge of things, deciding nightly on the river bank who did what. But now Fabrice was at the helm again. In charge of what would happen this night – he was going to fuck me, that was more than obvious. But there was a bigger thing than that. Which also became blindingly, wonderfully, obvious at this moment. He was in charge of what would happen to me not only now but for the rest of my life.

'To find you, lost and crying...' he said. But his own voice choked as he said it. He was lost and crying himself.

He fucked me very gently, and coaxed me off with his hand between our chests. It was after we'd both climaxed that I heard myself say it. In a whisper. 'I love you, Fabrice.'

*

We'd said the big thing. We said it several times again during that night. There were other things we'd need to say in due course – the fact that he had no luggage with him was just one among many things that had aroused my curiosity – but they could wait. For tonight we just pulled the duvet up over us and slept.

And in the morning Fabrice helped me into my socks.

Later we went out for coffee and a croissant. Not to the Little Horseshoe or the Figeac, where we'd run into people we knew. People who'd want explanations about things we hadn't yet explained to each other – or to ourselves. We went instead to the Kabylie, near place de la République, where I'd been with Joe. He'd be at work now. So would Antoine. Momo greeted me cheerfully when we arrived, but then left us in peace. We sat in the July sunshine outside on the pavement and began to talk.

'I found I couldn't go on living a lie for the rest of my life,' Fabrice was the first of us to confess.

I followed suit. 'I didn't even know I was living a lie,' I said. 'How lacking in self-knowledge can you get? But then you left Paris... You left me... And I found out about myself.'

'I'm so, so sorry,' Fabrice said quietly. 'To leave you...' His voice broke.

'Nothing to be sorry about,' I said. I clasped his hand beneath the table top. 'I never staked a claim to you. You weren't to know things about me that I was denying to myself. Oh Peter, Peter, Peter,' I said, tapping myself on the chest with each repetition of my own name. 'The man who three times denied the truth. I did it a hundred times more often. Can you forgive me for that?'

'My darling,' Fabrice said in English. 'My darling.' Tears spilled suddenly among his dark lashes and ran without ceremony down his cheeks. 'Thank you for not being hard on me,' he said. Then he had to stop until he'd composed himself. He went on at last, with a bit of difficulty, 'But you mustn't be hard on yourself either. You must learn to forgive yourself.'

For both of us that last thing was harder than you might think. For some days we went about with the feeling that we'd been cruel to each other. Actually, as time passed we began to see that we'd simply done what all people who love deeply have done at some point... Love is something that is always lived in a knife-drawer, and so it was going to be, we were discovering, with Fabrice and me. We had hurt each other very badly – but by accident.

*

But back to that first morning. The rest of our stories came out. Fabrice told me how he had left Régine. Learning I was about to become homeless had tipped the balance for him. He made a clean breast of it with her, he explained. He told her that he and I had been lovers. That he had been in love with me for some time, but had only just admitted it to himself. That he needed to tell her this before even checking with me to see if I felt the same. He didn't want to lie to her for even another minute. He had packed a bag and he caught the next train to Paris.

He knew he'd hurt her, and that pained him dreadfully. But in the end, he said, one had to be honest with other people, and with oneself.

When it came to hurting other people, I was luckier than he'd been. There had been no Régine in my case. I'd hurt myself and I'd hurt Fabrice, but there hadn't been anyone else within reach of my dishonesty and carelessness. Régine had said – when Fabrice announced his imminent departure – that she'd always known deep down about his gayness. She'd guessed also – hardly surprising, this – about me. I don't know if this made it better for Régine. At least it can't have made it worse.

There was another thing to deal with. Fabrice had arrived in the middle of the night without luggage, and with nowhere to stay except my small studio apartment, with its one single bed. I assumed this meant he'd lost his job or given it up. My apartment was mine only until the month's end, though. We'd both be out on our ears after that.

As for my own finances – well, you may have wondered how I was paying for my Paris lifestyle while attempting to burn with that hard gem-like flame and write. I'd been left a little money by a great aunt, actually, but it wouldn't last for ever. To tell the truth I was getting through it at a rate of knots. That first morning with Fabrice, sitting outside the Kabylie, I had to make a clean breast of that. 'But,' I told him, 'I'm OK with it if you are. I'm OK with you penniless if you're OK with me penniless.' Then I had to look down at my coffee cup, otherwise I'd have cried again. 'You're the only thing, the only person, I need or want, or have ever wanted in my entire life.' God knows how I managed to get all those words out.

'Look at me, Peter,' he said. With some difficulty I did. He took my chin in one of his hands gently, to stop me looking away again, I guess. 'That's all OK, then,' he said. 'You love me naked and without resources. I love you in the same way as that. Thank God.' Then he grinned at me. 'It's actually not quite so *dramatique*. I asked the bank if I could come back to Paris again at short notice. No, they weren't too happy about that. But they haven't fired me. They've re-posted me here in a smaller job, at a smaller salary. But it's liveable on. And the good news is they're letting me go back to the flat. We actually have somewhere to live. I dropped my baggage off there last night before I came to you. I went first to the Figeac but you weren't there. I got your door-code from Dominique.'

I took a deep breath. 'I'd still love you if you were a pauper,' I said. 'If we were both *clochards*. Share my last crust with you and all of that. And yet, if it doesn't come to that...'

He said, 'It hasn't come to that yet.' He looked up at the blue sky above us. 'We could walk in the sunshine for a bit, if you wanted to. After that, perhaps we can start moving your things into my apartment.'

In my mind's eye I saw at once those high ceilings, mirrors over the mantelpieces, friezes running around the walls... The big, big things in our lives can change so quickly sometimes. I could hardly believe any of what had happened in the last twelve hours. I was going to move into Fabrice's apartment. But that was only a little bit of it. The big thing was that I was going to share a home with Fabrice.

We were both startled at that moment to see Joe walking towards us along the street. He looked surprised to see us for a second. But then his expression changed. Reading his face as best I could, I thought I saw first wonder, then delight.

'Why aren't you at work?' I asked him when he came up.

'Just one of those days I happen to have no morning classes.' He shrugged. 'It sometimes just happens like that. On the other hand...' He looked enquiringly at me, then at Fabrice.

Fabrice didn't go into explanations. Not then, at any rate. He looked at Joe, and smiled at him, and said simply, 'I'm back for good.'

'For good?' Joe said. He grinned broadly. 'That's not good. That's not just *good*. That's the very, very best.'

*

The Paris Novel

It wasn't till autumn came and the evenings were getting dark that I remembered a story I'd never told Fabrice. I remembered it as we were making love one evening, naked, on the sofa, not prepared to wait (this was typical of us) until we got to bed. Carelessly we'd neglected to close the curtains or the blinds. I was on my back with Fabrice on top. Soon he would choose his moment to enter me, but we hadn't reached that point – the point after which philosophical discussion becomes impossible – quite yet. I glanced sideways towards the window. Beyond it, the yellow lights of other windows cut square holes in the blue night across the street. 'Van Gogh,' I said. 'Those windows in the dark.'

Fabrice stopped playing with my nipples for a moment. 'I see what you mean,' he said. Then he chuckled. 'Do you think anyone's out there watching us?'

I remembered suddenly my first evening in Paris. My peeping-Tom experience just hours before I met Fabrice. I told him now about that. Then I remembered the window that had so grabbed my imagination, opposite my old apartment in the rue des Archives. The question of who lived there, Joe had once suggested fancifully, was what had first brought me to France. The night Fabrice had left me, I'd had anxiety dreams about that...

I looked again at the yellow windows opposite. There was no sign of anyone. No silhouetted figures looking out. 'Do I think anyone's out there watching us?' I said. 'Can't say I'm sure, to be honest. But if they are, I'm fine with that, I think.'

Fabrice pushed his hard cock gently but firmly between my buttocks. 'I don't have any problem with that either,' he said. 'Not at the moment anyway. Tomorrow perhaps. But not tonight.'

Paris. September. 2013.

The sky is a cloudless blue. High overhead there are swallows passing over the city on their way south. I sit writing this in the gardens of the Tuileries. I am near the fountain pool by the great gates that open into the place de la Concorde. In the pool swim giant carp that seem almost as big as horses. Children who look smaller than the carp are sailing their boats across the top. Around me the flower beds are full of yellow and orange daisy-like flowers. There are hydrangeas and geraniums still, in fiercely clashing shades of pink and red.

Beyond the wall ahead of me stand the chestnut trees of the river bank. I smile at the memory of the person I was once, the crazed caged animal I was, wandering there so hungrily at night. I've never been back there in the last twenty-five years. Never felt the need.

Beyond the gates the top of the Eiffel Tower is visible. It looks different from day to day, according to my mood. Today it has something of the look about it of a medieval knight, benevolent and smiling. Magnificent in his plumed helmet. Gracious in the victory he has won at the joust.

In a little while Fabrice will join me, making a short detour from his work in the rue de Rivoli. We shall walk home together. Past the Louvre, past the Hôtel de Ville, then through the Marais to our flat. It's the same one that Fabrice had all those years ago, when it belonged to the bank.

It was probably lucky we had that conversation on that first morning of our new life together: the conversation about loving each other even if we were paupers. Because it nearly came to that. Fabrice lost his job in the banking fiasco of 2008. For a while we thought we'd be homeless. But the bank, keen just then to dispose of some fixed assets, offered to sell the apartment to us for a knock-down price. It wasn't that cheap, even so. Fabrice's father helped him. Even my own chipped in what he could.

We lived for a time on what I was earning as a magazine editor. (I still do that.) But then Fabrice set himself up on his own as a business consultant. That business has taken off in the last three years. Now we do all right.

We still frequent the Figeac. René runs it now, since his mother retired. And although Denis and Jeannette left Paris some years ago, we still see Marianne and Dominique. Also still together are Joe and Antoine, which is nice.

Another good thing is that Régine found love not long after splitting with Fabrice. With someone whose heterosexual credentials were less shaky than Fabrice's. He, Régine's husband, is Canadian. They live happily with their teenage children (as happily as anyone can live with teenage children, that is) in Alsace.

Françoise is another matter. She flew to the sun with the braceleted Portugueses guy all those years ago and, except for the one postcard, has never been heard of since. But she set her heart on what she wanted, and that is what she got. I've never felt sorry for her. There are many mansions in the house of love.

You don't have to be trapped by your past, I've learned. Life gives you more than one star among the heavens, as Dominique said. You can remove a domino or two from the tower without the whole thing collapsing about your ears. At least, that's what I now think.

Even the effects of frostbite – that numbness of the toes – disappeared after about a year and a half, though I thought during that time that it never would. The frostbite that afflicted my heart, though, the chill of the garden of the selfish giant, was dispelled in an instant, with the arrival of Fabrice at my bedroom door that night, with his return to Paris to stake his claim to outright ownership of my heart.

I never did become much of a writer. Except for my magazine stuff. Although the book I came to Paris to try and write ... well, you've just been reading it.

THE END

****

The Paris Novel

Anthony McDonald is the author of over twenty novels. He studied modern history at Durham University, then worked briefly as a musical instrument maker and as a farmhand before moving into the theatre, where he has worked in every capacity except director and electrician. He has also spent several years teaching English in Paris and London. He now lives in rural East Sussex.

Novels by Anthony McDonald
SILVER CITY

THE DOG IN THE CHAPEL

TOM & CHRISTOPHER AND THEIR KIND

RALPH: DIARY OF A GAY TEEN

IVOR'S GHOSTS

ADAM

BLUE SKY ADAM

GETTING ORLANDO

ORANGE BITTER, ORANGE SWEET

ALONG THE STARS

WOODCOCK FLIGHT

MATCHES IN THE DARK: 13 Tales of Gay Men

(Short story collection)

Anthony McDonald

Gay Romance Series:

Sweet Nineteen

Gay Romance on Garda

Gay Romance in Majorca

The Paris Novel

Gay Romance at Oxford

Gay Romance at Cambridge

The Van Gogh Window

Gay Tartan

Tibidabo

Spring Sonata

Touching Fifty

Romance on the Orient Express

All titles are available as Kindle ebooks and as paperbacks from Amazon.

www.anthonymcdonald.co.uk

Printed in Great Britain
by Amazon